GALLERIES OF JUSTICE

THE SIXTH CRYSTAL KINGDOM NOVEL

RAYMOND S FLEX

1

A FOOL'S ERRAND

S ULLIMAN couldn't hear himself think for the sound of his
own chattering teeth.

The chill in the cave was unbearable.

It cut him to the bone.

And yet Sully knew that he couldn't simply spark a fire into
life; he had done his best to try.

His best efforts had been met with abject failure.

Being unable to start a fire might've been acceptable, save for
the fact that nothing about his dress was suitable for the rigors of
such a quest as this.

When Louson Dorf—King of Shellacnass—had enlisted him
for this journey; into some godsforsaken land to the north of the
Kingdom, known only as the Winter's Moan; Sully hadn't had
much time to think about his dress; or what sort of equipment he
might need.

It had been something of a gallows-humoured game of Sully's

to make a mental itinerary of the equipment which he *would* have brought had he had full comprehension of what lay ahead:

A thick, sheepskin jacket.

That would've been the first item on his list.

A pair of solid, spiked boots for the ice.

Number two on the list.

Finally, and Sully thought of this as a *luxury* when compared to the first two, he enjoyed fantasising for brief moments about having brought along a nice, woollen hat.

One of those beautifully knitted jobs which he often saw on the market stalls of the Crystal Causeway in Ilsnare; the Crystal City.

As it was, Sully was stuck with his light, fair-weather tunic, a short summer jacket, designed only to ward off the *most minor* chills, and a pair of thinly woven trousers.

In short, the clothing which'd served him so well in his role as Sulliman, Royal Protector of the Plains, served him much less well now; in his role as Sully, Loyal Stooge to the King of Shellacnass.

Although Sully didn't begrudge Lou having sent him off on this quest—on this *fool's errand*—he wished that he might've been given a little more notice; and a *lot* more information on what he might be required to bring along.

But that was in the past now.

And *a lot* of good it would do him to witter on to himself about it.

That wouldn't help him get out alive.

Sully reached up and pulled his long black hair down over his eyes. Although he shook all over, he took the time to note, with a touch of self-deprecation, that he had more grey strands among the black since he'd left home. As his hands moved beyond the strands of hair, he felt the freezing-cold tips of his ears and he wondered whether or not frostbite might've set in. He hadn't had the presence of mind to bring a mirror along with him on this quest, although, it was fair to say, its need hadn't been so pressing as to make it into his mental list of his three *most* sought-after items.

He somehow managed a sigh through his constantly chattering teeth and he shifted his attention in the direction of his horse.

His horse lay on its side, its breathing heavy and disjointed; following no discernible rhythm. Its light-brown fur was covered in scabs. Pieces of its hide were missing; showing off the tough skin—or was it muscle and bone; a rib?—concealed beneath.

A gut-wrenchingly powerful stench filled the cave; one which put Sully in mind of rotting flesh.

Most likely it *was* rotting flesh.

Back when Sully had been a boy, well over thirty, forty summers ago—if he could believe it—he had had a job in a butcher's shop.

He hadn't been entrusted with cutting the meat.

No, as Sully soon learned throughout his abridged apprenticeship, the cutting of meat was a delicate art which took years to master . . . or to even be *competent* at.

The butcher had tasked Sully with the ignoble task of fishing through the salted storage—the large wooden containers inside of which hunks of meat were preserved. Sully's job was to search for any meat which had maggots already crawling out from it. Anything short of animal life was pronounced fair game for sale and consumption.

And, goodness, Sully had found some *dreadful* specimens throughout the years.

In fact, it sent a fresh shudder through him just to think about it.

He turned his attention away from his whimsical—and, no doubt, *dewy-eyed*—recollections, and back to his horse.

The best-case scenario, as he had judged it, was that his horse would be dead by morning.

There was nothing for Sully to do about that.

He cast his mind to how it had happened—to how he had *let* himself get into such a tight spot.

A day or so earlier, he had ridden clean away from the fields filled with endless grazing cattle and mutton; had left behind the swaying, tall, green grass; and said a very reluctant goodbye to the sun.

He, and his horse, had crossed over onto the permafrost.

Although Sully had felt the dizzying effects of the altitude as he had travelled higher and higher, up the spiralling track, further into the Winter's Moan, he hadn't been able to square the fearsome reputation which the region commanded throughout the Kingdom.

Often, in his childhood, and even to this day, parents would threaten their children with the prospect of being sent to the Winter's Moan if they failed to finish their dinner; if they refused to complete their house chores . . . as far as Sully could remember, his parents would regularly use the grim concept of the Winter's Moan to get him out of the house and into work; whichever job that happened to be at the time.

Now, though, having travelled a full day into the Winter's

Moan, Sully had come to realise just *why* it had acquired notoriety.

He supposed that high spirits—some childish sense of adventure—had been to blame for his earlier overconfidence. He'd wondered at how, despite the screaming gales, and the ice which spat down on them, his horse had easily kept its footing; its hooves somehow finding a firm grip through the soft layer of snow to the hard ice beneath.

Before Sully had ventured into the Winter's Moan, he *had* had the good sense to visit a blacksmith so that his horse would have proper shoes for the task ahead.

He felt slightly aggrieved that the blacksmith hadn't thought to advise him on his own clothing at all . . . but perhaps the blacksmith had not thought it his place; not his *job* to do so.

Sully, after all, was a grown man; and, in theory, capable of making decisions which affected his own health and wellbeing.

A reason which had brought him here.

As he had turned the corner into the hillside, he recalled feeling his horse slip.

At first, he had thought nothing of it at all. His horse had slipped many times on their journey through the Winter's Moan; often losing traction for several seconds before, all at once, refinding the balance which'd previously eluded it. Most of the times it had occurred, he had put the matter down to his horse finding its way across the icy terrain.

Like himself, Sully believed the horse to be unfamiliar with snowy conditions and so still becoming accustomed to the sensation.

But this time it'd been different.

His horse had never found the sure ground beneath the snow and ice.

It had slipped, and slid, and *kept* moving . . .

Sully could remember, quite clearly, being ready to throw himself off the back of the horse; to tumble down onto the snow below, but the force at which he had been moving made it impossible.

He had simply stuck to the saddle, unable to prevent himself falling with the horse.

From then on, all he could recall was falling and falling; being unable to stop it.

He recalled seeing the sky, up above him, a sort of wispy grey shade.

The sun nothing more than a brightness in the cloud beyond.

He and his horse had tumbled down between sheets of ice, and then come to rest here—with a hard *thump*—in what had turned out to be a cave.

Somehow, as Sully had felt himself about to hit the floor, he had twisted his body.

Managed to land on his haunches; to take most of the force of the fall.

To absorb the shock.

The worst he had to show for it was a pain in his left ankle.

His horse, though, had been a different story.

He glanced over at his horse again now, seeing it lying on its side and wishing there might be something he could do to ease its suffering . . .

He knew—from looking up to the sky from where he had fallen—that there was a chance of him being able to escape; but none for his horse.

And, watching the clouds turning from their wispy white to an ashen grey, he knew that night would be here soon. The whole cave—this *crevice* in the rock—would be steeped in darkness.

With a long-held sigh, Sully turned his attention back to the horse and to the saddlebags.

He could try to light another fire.

Most likely he was going to spend the night in this cave.

It was the safest place for him now.

Because there was no way of knowing what might be outside.

Wolves?

Bears?

He didn't want to think about it.

All he hoped was—whatever predatory animals there might be outside—they wouldn't be able to clamber down here.

2

INTERROGATION

FLUCKNOR could hardly keep himself still.

It felt almost as if he might bake in his *skin* from the anxiety which rushed through him.

He glanced back up at the clock.

Saw, again, just how long it was past midday.

He thought about how he'd had his blond hair trimmed this morning by a member of the Ilsnare Palace house staff. He could still feel a few loose hairs, which'd escaped the hairdresser's coarse brush, itching the back of his neck.

And then there was the getup he'd been forced to dress in this morning—what he wore now: the flowing, emerald-green robes.

He looked just like any other of the many Representatives who swarmed about here; about the Galleries of Justice. All of them in their multi-coloured robes.

Louson Dorf; King of Shellacnass, had seen fit to hand him the position of High Representative.

A job which Flucknor, and everyone else, although they dared not say it in front of the King, knew that Flucknor was ill-suited for.

He was patently two decades—*at least!*—too young.

And he had none of the years of study which were required for Representatives.

Those things aside, he had heard the gossip about his humble upbringing; about how he hadn't even been born in Ilsnare, and —*shock of all shocks!*—that he was a lapsed monk.

That he had left Ravensbark behind in order to join Louson Dorf.

As some—unkindly—put it: to lend *moral* support to Louson Dorf's throne.

But Lou had insisted on Flucknor accepting the role of High Representative, and when Lou set his mind to some idea or other there wasn't usually a way to convince him otherwise.

Gods help him, certainly Flucknor had *tried.*

Flucknor turned his attention back to the expansive, mahogany double doors which led to the room where the Council of Wisemen sat.

Of course they knew just as well as everyone else how poor of a choice Flucknor would be as High Representative. That was why they were keeping him waiting.

To be honest, Flucknor supposed he would've done the same thing in the Council of Wisemen's position. Why should *they* pander to some pretender . . . no matter whether or not it was the King who had declared them?

Finally, Flucknor heard the hinges of the double doors emit a *creak* and he turned to look.

A manservant appeared.

He was dressed in copper-coloured robes; the robes of those who served the Council of Wisemen.

He gave Flucknor a slight smirk, and Flucknor was certain that the manservant, like everyone else, had already taken his turn to poke fun at the ridiculousness of the situation.

Even *he*—a humble *manservant*—could tell that Flucknor wasn't fit to be the High Representative.

Flucknor rose up off the wooden bench where he'd been sitting. He walked in through the doorway; passing by the manservant.

The first thing which struck Flucknor about the room where the Council of Wisemen sat was the large window which looked out over the rooftops of Ilsnare; the Crystal City.

He drank in the view, how the sunlight glistened off the glass rooftops; sending a slightly painful sensation into the back of Flucknor's eyeballs.

He had ice magic running in his veins, and although Lou had promised to teach him more about his abilities, he had noted that his role had become more of a *confidante* than any sort of protégé. In fact, Flucknor couldn't recall the last time Lou had sat him down and spoken to him about any matter of import . . . anything which concerned the *Magical*.

Sometimes Flucknor felt frustrated, as if Lou was intentionally hiding a whole world from him; a world which, if Flucknor truly wished it, he could reach out and take.

Flucknor's vision slowly drifted back to the foreground, where he took in the seven members of the Council of Wisemen.

All seven of them sat about the well-polished mahogany table, their hands invariably clasped before them; their lips pert. Their eyes all fixed on Flucknor.

Each of them wore golden robes over the top of crimson tunics.

They looked *quite* majestic with their grey heads of hair, their leathered, well-worn skin and their generally wizen expressions.

Certainly far more majestic than Flucknor.

He wondered if he was supposed to sit down at the table, like them, or if he was supposed to keep on standing here like a lemon.

Flucknor had never been at all good at public speaking and he felt his chest tightening now; as if some invisible hands were reaching around him from behind and attempting to squeeze all the air from his lungs.

In the end, one of the Council of Wisemen put him out of his misery.

And, as it turned out, it wasn't a wise *man* at all, but a woman.

"Good morning," she said. "My name is Leona."

Like the other members of the Council of Wisemen, the woman had grey hair.

But her skin was youthful looking; free of wrinkles.

Deciding that he was supposed to address his attention to *Leona*, Flucknor did so.

"I was told to come here," Flucknor said, "so that I might be sworn in?"

Even as the words floated out through his lips, he could hear them twisting and turning on him; losing their power . . . sounding as if he was a kid again.

And, in this company, he really did feel like a kid.

Leona gave him a professional smile, and then glanced about the room. "We've been speaking among ourselves and, as I'm sure you will have no doubt overheard among some quarters, there's been some, uh . . . *discussion* as to whether you might be the appropriate person for this role." She narrowed her eyes slightly. "You do understand what duties the High Representative must abide by?"

The way that she left it open for Flucknor to answer—as a *question*—sent a skitter up his spine.

He felt his heart bounce about his chest for a couple of beats and then he reminded himself that Lou was the one who'd hand-picked him for this role . . . and surely that had to count for something.

Surely Lou had seen something in him which nobody else had.

That said, Flucknor really didn't know how to reply to Leona.

The best answer he could come up with was that he *superficially* understood the role of High Representative; in that the High Representative worked as a sort of go-between for the Galleries of Justice and the Council of Wisemen; a kind of mediator.

Flucknor couldn't see, for himself, why *he* would be particularly suited for this role; but, again, it wasn't like it was his decision to make.

Leona—*apparently*—took Flucknor's silence—*correctly*—as a sign that he *hadn't* quite grasped the intricacies of the role of High Representative.

She glanced about the Council of Wisemen, and, in profile, Flucknor caught her arching an eyebrow. When she turned back to Flucknor, she had a slight smirk clinging to her lips. "Listen, I think this is what we shall do." She breathed in deeply, and then exhaled. "Since we, unfortunately, have our doubts about appointing you to the role of High Representative—given your lack of education in this respect, your lack of *experience*—we propose, owing to the King's recommendation, and until such a time as we can confirm the King's wishes, that we make you interim High Representative." She stopped, apparently finished. Then smiled widely. "How does that sound?"

For several seconds, Flucknor felt dazed, as if all those beady eyes were waiting for something from him. And he knew that they were.

They wanted his reply.

They wanted to hear from the *King*.

Again, Flucknor's throat felt dry, but this time he managed to get a little more power into his words, enough so that his voice didn't break completely as he spoke. "Look," he began, "I'm as doubtful about this as the rest of you, but the King has made it clear that this is what he wants—what're we supposed to do?"

Leona smiled back at him. "Well, I *suppose* that one of us should try to convince him."

Flucknor shook his head.

Leona's smile faltered.

"No," Flucknor responded, "believe me, I've tried; he was adamant that I should be appointed as High Representative . . . he even went through the process of meeting with several other candidates; others which, believe me, would've been far more suitable. But, in the end, he stated plainly and clearly that he wanted *me* to be the High Representative."

The room descended into a stony silence.

Flucknor longed to break it, and yet, at the same time, he felt as if a growing weight was forming across his shoulders, pushing him down into the floor.

Forcing him to remain on the spot where he now stood.

Finally, Leona was the one who broke the silence.

"So," she said, "what should we *do*?"

Flucknor glanced about the room.

He could see no solution to the problem, although the choice was quite plain; the Council of Wisemen could go against the King's wishes . . . or they could simply humour him.

3

THE SOORE WHIP

FLUCKNOR scuttled through the backstreets of the Crystal City, hearing his footsteps reverberating off the walls about him.

In the air, he could smell the strong scent of the unsold, day-old fish, being tossed into the River Ils by the fish mongers.

His throat still felt dry, despite the fact that he had knocked back copious glasses of water before leaving the Galleries of Justice following his meeting with the Council of Wisemen.

He was the new High Representative.

Not even *provisionally*.

His appointment was official.

He could still clearly recall the cold, dead handshakes he had received from the Council of Wisemen by way of congratulations on accepting his new role, and he couldn't quite shake the feeling that every last one of the Wisemen would be on the lookout for any reason—*any reason at all*—to strip him of his duties.

Any reason to boot him out onto the street.

Which was where he surely belonged.

Wrapped in his thick, chocolate-brown, fleecy overcoat, which stretched down to his ankles, he reached out and rapped his knuckles against the sturdy oak door in the back alley of *The Soore Whip.*

Tonight there was a meeting and Flucknor, as always, would be in attendance.

Remembering himself, Flucknor glanced about, seeing if there was anybody watching on. When he saw that there wasn't, he reached up for his hood and brought it down so that it would conceal his face.

He waited for a few moments and then, when the door opened, felt himself scrutinised by the single eyeball concealed within the hood of the sable cloak.

Like always, the door pulled back into the tavern and the implication was that Flucknor was to enter. Which he did.

Once Flucknor stood inside the tavern, he felt the gentle, warming glow of the stove embering away unseen within the bar area.

Deeper into the tavern, Flucknor imagined Fhan—the proprietor—with his squat, round body behind the bar serving pints to all those who had the grung to pay for it . . . a publican never could be too careful in a zone of the city such as this one; there were plenty of chancers who would nip in for a pint with the idea of snatching it up and downing it before any money had changed hands.

Flucknor turned his attention back to the corridor before him.

Even on warm, long, late-spring nights, such as this one, he enjoyed the sensation of entering a well-heated abode.

Tonight, following the meeting, he might even allow himself a honey ale.

He *was* supposed to be celebrating his appointment to High Representative, after all . . . if he played his cards right, Fhan might even serve him one on the house.

Flucknor turned and took in the cloaked figure who had allowed him access.

Although the cloaked figure didn't pull down his hood, Flucknor knew precisely who it was:

Rintersyart; a Cyclops.

The Creature who always stood at the back door, monitoring those who came and went; doing what he could to weed out those who either looked to start trouble or who might wish to expose the inner-workings of the movement.

Flucknor reached out and clasped Rintersyart firmly on the shoulder. "I've got news," Flucknor said. "But it can wait until afterwards—will you stick around?"

Rintersyart gave Flucknor a firm nod.

Flucknor released him from his hold and set on his way, through the back corridors of the tavern, headed for the room which was kept reserved for the Creatures' meetings.

Every time that Flucknor returned here, for the meetings, he found himself thinking about how he had first begun attending in the service of the Eye—the vast spy network which extended throughout the Kingdom of Shellacnass and of which Louson Dorf, the King, was the leader.

Several of the many—*many*—advisors of the Eye had suggested that Lou might want to have a few spies concentrate on meetings of so-called 'subversives' . . . those who might plan to disturb the status quo within Ilsnare; the Crystal City.

And one particular category which fell beneath this definition was the Creatures, who were, at this moment and time, vying for recognition—for *freedom* and *equality*— in the Mortal world.

Freedom and equality which the Council of Wisemen, and the Kingdom of Shellacnass in general, saw fit to deny them. And had done for the past decades; since before Flucknor was born.

Having magical blood running through his veins, Flucknor found the arguments in these meetings fascinating. And he was sure Lou, being an ice mage himself, would have also been extremely interested if he'd found himself in Flucknor's position . . . if he hadn't had to maintain his noble position as *King*.

That said, Flucknor most definitely did not speak to Lou about the meetings he attended these days. He had long ago moved beyond his work for the Eye and he could now honestly state—if there ever came a time when he'd be forced to—that he came to these meetings only because of his personal beliefs.

Of course, in his new role as High Representative, he would have to take care. He knew that since he now held a public office, he could be held accountable for his personal views. But, then again, he didn't plan on making a song and dance about his attendance of these meetings.

Once inside the small back room of *The Soore Whip*, he eyed the five cloaked figures who all stood up on the stage. Without so much as a moment's hesitation, he trod his way up the wooden steps and arrived alongside them.

He looked to the faces, concealed beneath the hoods, in the flickering torchlight. He saw that they all had the same rash-red complexion. The same scabs and horns growing out from the surface of the skin. The same *black* eyes.

The long, lizard-like snouts.

Horrox, each and every one of them.

But whereas many of the Horrox prided themselves in working within the system—using their shapeshifting abilities to make themselves *appear* Mortal; just as the former butler Tineoots Pottler had done—the ones here were only interested in being able to walk through the streets of the Crystal City in their true forms.

No longer did they want to skulk in the shadows.

And Flucknor couldn't rightly blame them.

Before he could say anything at all, the leader of the meeting —Brotsboore—took a step forward; toward Flucknor. Already, Flucknor could sense something in the air.

On another occasion, he might've termed it *tension* . . . and yet, these evening meetings—when the Creatures gathered together to further their efforts for seizing hold of freedom—were the only time when Flucknor *truly* felt he was himself.

Why should he feel nervous here?

Brotsboore reached up and laid his clawed hand on Flucknor's shoulder.

Flucknor felt the reptilian bone structure against his skin.

And it made him feel greatly uneasy.

Brotsboore eased Flucknor away from the other cloaked figures—away from the other Horrox. He led Flucknor back down off the stage.

This made Flucknor feel even *more* uneasy.

When Flucknor looked to the stage, he saw that the other Horrox had all turned in among themselves—their backs to Flucknor and Brotsboore . . . speaking about who knew what?

"What's the matter?" Flucknor said, shifting his attention to Brotsboore and deciding that he needed to break the silence.

Brotsboore attempted a smile, but it came out as more of a smirk. " 'The matter' ?" he said, and then his smirk widened. "*Nothing's* the matter. In fact, quite the opposite. I believe that congratulations should be in order."

These words might've meant something to Flucknor if it hadn't been for the deadpan tone with which Brotsboore delivered them.

Flucknor could tell something was wrong.

Really wrong.

He wheedled his way out from beneath Brotsboore's grasp and then he peered back into those inky, pit-black eyes. "Is this because I've been appointed High Representative?" he said. "You don't want me here anymore—is that the reason?"

Brotsboore pursed his lizard-like lips and then he tilted his head to one side. "You must understand, Flucknor, that our mission is larger than any one member of the group; and that great pains must be taken so that it shall be ensured. So that any danger to its success might be minimised as well as possible."

Flucknor glanced back at the stage. He caught one of the cloaked figures looking, and the cloaked figure responded by turning away as swiftly as he could.

He turned back to Brotsboore. "Listen," Flucknor said, lowering his tone now, "I'm here to fight your corner, now that I've got some power—*real power*—I can help to push forward the issue; to help the cause. To make equality—*freedom*—for all Magical beings a reality. And not just throughout Ilsnare but the whole Kingdom. The *whole* of Shellacnass."

Brotsboore wouldn't even allow Flucknor to finish before he was shaking his head vigorously. "No, Flucknor, I'm afraid not."

Now Flucknor was certain that he felt a slight *tingle* in the air . . . that static charge of magic. He knew that, unlike mages—Mortals who carried magic in their blood—Creatures could not control their magic so easily. It was more an intrinsic part of their makeup.

As unshiftable as the pattern of one's palm.

Brotsboore's stubbornness—his anger?—was leaking from his body through his magic.

Flucknor knew that he had to take care. Although it was true to say that he had magic running through his own blood, his own mastery was certainly not up to protecting himself from rogue magic—especially that as strong as the Horrox might produce.

If only Lou, or his sister—*Syre*—had been here . . . but neither of them were.

Brotsboore went on. "We tried for so long—my *race* tried for so long to function within the Mortal world . . . and now it's time for a difference. We must cast off all those who seek to work within the system, because the system itself is broken."

The static charge in the air reached its peak.

Flucknor felt all the hairs stand up on his arms.

Finally, when it felt as though a bolt of magic might shoot through Flucknor's throat, the static shifted. It became less pronounced.

Weaker.

And then it was almost gone completely.

"Do you understand?" Brotsboore replied. "Do you understand why we can't have you here?"

Flucknor stared long and hard into Brotsboore's beady black eyes, and he saw compassion mixed in there, among the fatigue and the unwillingness to wait any longer for a revolution to take place.

Flucknor's throat felt constricted. He knew he wouldn't be able to make so much as a sound when he opened his mouth. So he nodded in reply.

Yes, he understood.

Brotsboore reached up and laid his hand on Flucknor's shoulder once more, and then gave him an almost fatherly squeeze. "Take care, Flucknor," he said. "And goodbye."

4

DAWNING

S ULLY STIRRED when he felt the sunlight on the backs of his eyelids.

For several seconds, he stared through the webbed veins; the redness filling his vision.

Finally, he opened his eyes.

The scene was just like it had been in his dreams, which was to say—in a word—*hopeless.*

The first detail which Sully noticed was how his horse lay very still, its ribs not even rising any longer. Its whole body having gone stiff.

So much for *riding* his way out of this crevice.

Sully rose up off the cave floor, leaving the hard—but thankfully *unfrozen*—ground beneath him.

He stretched his aching arms upward, feeling as if he'd been hurled down the side of a mountain while he'd slept . . . then again, he supposed that wasn't so far from the truth.

He recalled how, whenever he went on long rides, or whenever he was called upon to take some long walking journey, he would feel pain dancing all over his body the day after.

Sully turned his attention to his sad efforts at a fire the previous night.

He had just about managed to locate some nearby rocks, large enough to mark out the campfire, but there had been no kindling to go with his tinderbox, or, for that matter, any loose, dry branches.

Still, the night was over now; the sun had risen.

The time for a fire had passed . . . unless Sully wished to have a cooked breakfast, that was.

Despite his aches and pains, and how Sully felt as if his entire body had been frozen solid in the night, he shifted over to his dead horse. He fished through the saddlebags, turning up whatever he could from within. Some food, extra clothing, more tinderboxes.

As he dug through the contents of the saddlebags, he couldn't help but note that there seemed to be nothing at all which would aid his efforts to climb his way out of this crevice.

He tilted his head back to look again.

To examine the long way up . . . back to the mountain path.

Last night, he had been so preoccupied with exhaustion and desperation to light a fire that his escape had seemed an almost secondary concern.

Now, though, in the cruel light of day, he saw that it was going to be a *huge* undertaking.

As he scanned the jagged rocks which stuck out from the walls, he noted how it seemed to be volcanic in makeup; easily flaked off if he were to put the strain of his weight on one part in particular.

Sully glanced about himself, hopeful that he might find some crack in the rock where he might be able to squeeze himself through; where he might be able to make his escape by foot without even *having* to climb up the rock face.

But there was nothing.

Only the cave surrounding him.

The single way out above his head.

Sully allowed himself a single sigh, and a final look through the saddlebags before he knew that there was nothing for it. That he would need to clamber his way out of here; hand over hand; one step at a time.

On the positive side, it was still early in the morning.

He had all day to try and make his escape.

And a whole day to wallow in disappointment . . .

5

AWAY FROM US

A S FLUCKNOR trudged through the night-time streets of Ilsnare, he heard the gentle, throbbing beat of music coming from the taverns; the drunken laughter of friends forged in ale.

He could smell the thick scent of ale on the air, and, rather than it seeming inviting—as it had done when he'd first set foot in *The Soore Whip* this evening—it now seemed to have taken on an almost acrid quality. It turned his stomach just to think about it.

Flucknor couldn't quite shift the childlike feeling of rejection which afflicted him. That sense of being an outsider he would experience whenever other children excluded him from their games.

He recalled the day when the monks had come to his village of Dweldwock; and how they had given him those strange facial expressions when they'd passed him by.

Somehow, Flucknor hadn't felt surprised, he had always

known that he was different from the others who inhabited his village. That he was different from his mother and father.

Neither of his parents understood that he had ice magic flowing through his veins . . . although his mother might've had more than a sneaking suspicion . . . after all, the only explanation for Flucknor's Magical qualities could've been from the intervention of a travelling mage . . .

When his parents had come to him and asked him whether he would like to go with the monks—whether he would like to become one of them—there had been no question in Flucknor's mind.

He knew that his desire to leave was equal to his parents' desire for him not to stay.

And so he had gone.

His childhood in Ravensbark had been otherworldly; in many different meanings of the word. For one, he had met with others, like him, with magic flowing through their veins; others who'd been rejected by their families, almost all of them surely the results of extra-marital affairs . . . the mixture of Magical blood with Mortal.

Although the monks lived with magic every day—magic flowed beneath everything like a subterranean river—it was a question of suppressing rather than a matter of embracing. Their charge—as monks—was to maintain balance within the Magical world . . .

Their abstinence from magic would hold the world together.

Stop it from coming apart at the seams.

Keep any one of the Four Corners of the Magical Field from overwhelming the other:

Fire.

Ice.

Light.

Dark.

The monks' duty was to sit in the middle.

To *not* pick a side.

Strange to think that, even a decade after he had left the monastery at Ravensbark, Flucknor still hadn't nailed himself down to any one Corner. He supposed that the value of remaining neutral to all disputes—to upholding abstinence—had been well engrained into his very being . . . so much so that he could no longer separate it from himself.

From his own beliefs.

Now, though, he supposed his distance from magic would allow him a perspective not afforded those more afflicted; those like Lou, or Brotsboore.

Wasn't that one of the key assets which was required in a High Representative?

That they remain indifferent to either side; that they provide the simple facts between the King of Shellacnass and the Council of Wisemen?

Flucknor only realised where he was when he glanced up.

The Crystal Causeway.

The Crystal Causeway ran alongside the River Ils and wound up through the bundled-together townhouses to Ilsnare Palace itself.

Now that he noted the slick, greenish surface of the river running alongside him, he caught up with the pungent smell of the water; thick with sewage, and those rotten fish which he'd seen the mongers throwing out earlier.

He spotted several rats scampering about the muddy banks of

the river, dipping their hind paws into the water and snatching at the morsels which passed by.

Pigeons too.

All the scavengers were out tonight.

On instinct, Flucknor turned his attention to the pit-black City Walls which ran around the circumference of the city; and then to the City Gates at the end of the Crystal Causeway.

He thought long and hard about what to do next.

Perhaps he should go and check.

It would be a simple, quick trip out through the City Gates to the knot in the nearby tree stump.

Most likely there wouldn't be anything there—there wouldn't be any parchment.

Whenever he had gone to check, once or twice in the past week, there'd been no further message from the exiled Syre. At one point, she had been writing to him, leaving notes in the agreed spot, once a week . . . now, though, they had become so infrequent as to be classified a rare occurrence.

Just to think of Syre, to imagine her dark hair; her glittering *eyes.*

The chill of her ice magic whenever he brushed so much as a fingertip up against her skin.

There really wasn't time for his mind to wander. He had matters to attend to. Much to get done in his new role. Yes, he should return to the Palace, it would be a real mess if—

"Flucknor! Flucknor Arch!"

Flucknor turned, not recognising the voice.

He squinted long and hard into the gloom; just about held at bay by the twitching flicker of the torchlight.

He eyed the figure, hobbling along, his face obscured by his cloak hood.

Flucknor reached into his own cloak, feeling the handle of his dagger there.

He often practised the action of slipping it from its scabbard.

Practised slashing it through the air.

If he needed to attack he would do just that.

Slowly, Flucknor read the details in the stranger's face.

And he realised that he wasn't a stranger at all.

It was Damon Shriversmyth.

6

THE GHOST OF RAVENSBARK

A NUMBNESS crept across the surface of Flucknor's skin.

For several long moments, Flucknor was certain that he was toppling backward; that he was going to fall—hit the cobblestones hard and be knocked unconscious.

But then he retained something of his inner-strength.

And he forced himself to stand up to the man who had once been his Abbot at Ravensbark.

Damon Shriversmyth.

"Come a little closer, lad," Damon said, "so that I might see you better."

Flucknor didn't move for several seconds.

The numbness which passed over the surface of his skin was replaced by a prickling sensation. As if somebody danced a thousand invisible needles across his body.

Damon's appearance was so different to how Flucknor

would've pictured it in his mind's eye; completely at odds to how he *imagined* him.

Gone were his round, chubby cheeks.

The loose lips.

And—most striking of all—the *hulking* size.

Why, before, Damon had towered over Flucknor.

He had towered over *everyone*.

Now, though, Damon had a hunchback. He walked with a cane; his crooked spine arched over as he stood in the gloom.

Damon reached up and brought his hood down across his shoulders.

Whereas before, Damon had had thick, lusty, mousy-brown hair, now he was almost bald, with only a pair of wispy grey tufts of hair jutting out from the sides of his scalp.

Flucknor might've passed him in the street a thousand times and thought nothing of it.

Just another stranger.

"My," Damon said, reaching out to touch Flucknor on the cheek, "you really have grown into yourself, haven't you, son?"

There was the old term of address, the one which Flucknor had grown so accustomed to during his time at Ravensbark as an apprentice. And, almost as if it was a knee-jerk reflex, he replied to Damon in the expected manner. "Yes, father," Flucknor said.

This brought a smile onto Damon's withered face, and then a throaty chuckle from out between the cracked lips. Flucknor was taken aback to smell ale on the old man's breath. Damon shook his head. "No need for that now, lad," he replied. "I'm not Abbot anymore, as you might have guessed."

Now that Flucknor got a better look at Damon in the torch-light of the Crystal Causeway, he could see that, indeed, Damon was dressed in a mulchy-brown coloured cloak—the cloak which was most often seen worn by hobblesmen; the men who wandered from place to place, plagued by magic, or memories, or both; tormented by the world and unable to find rest.

But how had this happened to Damon?

To his Father Abbot?

Damon had been such a *solid* individual, he had been the one who'd faced off with countless mages, maintained the sanctity for as long as he could at Ravensbark . . . until Ma'reygar and his magical army had arrived to bring it tumbling to the ground.

Damon had done his level best to adjudicate disputes within the Magical community, and, more often than not, he had managed to avoid great injustices; seemingly irrepressible violence.

To see him like this—a *hobblesman*—almost broke Flucknor's heart.

Unable to think of anything else to do, Flucknor shrugged off his overcoat and then draped it about Damon's shoulders.

Although Damon parted his lips, apparently to protest, his shuddering was so pronounced that not so much as a sound was produced.

"This way," Flucknor said, somehow—from *somewhere*—able to produce a smile as he gestured Damon in the direction of Ilsnare Palace, up along the Causeway. "You'll be surprised to see how far I've come. And I'm sure that Lou would be delighted to see you."

7

ANOTHER FAILURE

SULLY PRESSED his back against the rigid rock face.
He felt the uneven surface of the rock through his too-thin tunic.

If his body had ached before, then the sensation he felt right now was pure—*unadulterated*—pain.

The sunlight had long ago passed away overhead, and he could feel the twilight already giving way to night.

The stench of his decaying horse was revolting and yet he didn't have the strength to so much as reach up and cover his mouth and nostrils with his hand; or to use one of his spare tunics to breathe through.

What was the point of easing his discomfort? It was only temporary and, anyway, it worked as a sort of physical proof that he was still alive; a reminder that he wasn't dead yet.

Once he ceased to smell the rotting remains of his horse, he would know he was dead.

And he would be dead soon.

He felt like a failure; there was no getting away from that.

He had spent the entire day clambering up the rock face, doing his best to get to the surface.

But he hadn't been able to get so much as a quarter of the way up before his hands had begun to shake; before his fingers began to feel as if they had caught fire.

And he'd been forced to let go.

To drop back down to the ground.

Each time Sully had picked himself up off the cave floor, ventured his way back up the rock face another time, he felt his muscles begin to shudder and then give way. And his mind had told him that he couldn't.

There was nothing he could do about it.

He *would* die here.

He peered up through the gap in the crevice above him, and he saw the moon sweep into view. It was hard to imagine that this was the same moon he had seen throughout his life; that it was the same moon which'd shone down on him when he'd been a child; when he'd become a skuller; and then when he'd stood by Lou's side and helped to ward off the most powerful—certainly the most *evil*—wizard of their times.

A sad end, indeed, that he would die of thirst, or starvation, in the heart of the Winter's Moan.

But, in a way, he supposed it was appropriate.

He had never had a chance to play the hero, and he wouldn't do so now.

He would die the death he deserved.

That of the right-hand man.

As Sully thought over his life, and what he had done with it, he could at least say that there had been a certain drama. The last ten years, true, had been somewhat dreary by comparison; he hadn't experienced anything like the adventures he'd had while he'd been at Lou's side.

But he could say one thing with near certainty, that he wouldn't be having any more adventures at Lou's side in the future.

Not in this world.

Feeling the tug of hunger and thirst becoming almost unbearable, Sully allowed his eyelids to droop; so that he might block out the moonlight which drifted down from above, into the crevice.

He didn't want to see his horse; that ill omen, all laid out before him.

How *he* would look in a matter of weeks, days . . . hours?

When Sully first felt that static charge of magic in the air, he believed that he had drifted off to sleep. That his brain had allowed him the luxury of dreams while the rest of him began to submit to death.

It was only when he opened his eyes wide, when he glanced all around himself, that he realised that a faint, lime-green light now illuminated the cave.

It illuminated the horse's carcass.

Sully's chest tightened, not from hope, but out of anticipation.

He supposed that if he'd had to narrow down the feeling even further then he might've described the sensation as something akin to *fear* . . .

One thing was for certain, from all the magic he had seen performed throughout his life, it had only impressed terror upon him—of what it was capable of; of the many ways it could inflict pain on Mortals. Even though he considered Lou a lifelong friend, he always felt a slight sense of fear being in his company; knowing that Lou, if he wished, could tear Sully apart—piece by piece . . . and leave nothing left.

Not that he ever would, of course.

The lime-green light in the cave was too strong for Sully to bear. He brought his forearm up to shield his eyes. His whole body seized tight and he felt a slight nausea swirling in his gut.

A minute might've passed before Sully felt that it was safe for him to bring his forearm down; for him to look out on whatever Magical terror had made its presence felt here.

He felt an aching sense of irony that he had allowed himself to slip into the belief that the Winter's Moan wasn't anywhere near as terrible as society—as the whole of *Shellacnass*—would have him believe . . . from what he had experienced in the past day or so, it was all that and *worse*.

His overconfidence would cost him his life.

The lime-green light wasn't as bright as it had been previously; it was now reduced to a faint glow. Sully wondered if the intensity of the light had let off or if his eyes had simply grown accustomed to it.

When he finally swept his gaze about the cave, he came to a halt upon the Creature which now stood before him.

Floppy, velvety ears; almost like a rabbit's, but grey.

All its skin was grey.

It had spry limbs and a protruding, smooth stomach.

Large, round eyes.

If Sully had been standing, it would've barely reached his waist.

He wondered at what it might be.

Goblin?

Gremlin?

Some sort of *sprite*?

Finally, as if Sully had prompted the Creature with his thoughts, it spoke to him.

Within his mind:

— *A Glyph.*

"Excuse me?" Sully replied, blurting out the words, his own voice sounding strange—*alien.*

He had truly believed that he would never hear his voice again . . . at least not in conversation with another person. With another *thing.*

This time the sprite repeated itself aloud:

"A Glyph," it said.

Sully blinked several times, the lime-green glow now becoming as second nature to him as the daylight. He stared long and hard at the 'Glyph' and wondered at all the stories he had been told throughout the years; all the ones which parents *continued* to tell their children.

About all the Creatures which didn't *really* exist.

This one, though, unless it was some sort of end-of-life delusion, *did.*

"What . . . where," Sully said, glancing about himself, and realising that there was nothing except for the Glyph standing at centre stage; before him. Finally he got his thoughts together and managed to untangle his tongue. "Where did you come from?"

The Glyph eyed Sully for several moments, and then tilted its head upward, to the gap above their heads, and the moonlight beyond. When the Glyph turned its attention back to Sully, it had a slight smile smeared all over its lips. "You fell down here, didn't you?"

Sully found himself lost for several moments.

Then he regained himself.

"Yes," he replied, his answer short, succinct.

He parted his lips to add something else before deciding that he didn't *have* anything else to add.

The Glyph eyed Sully closely, its smile widening further. "Would you like to get out?"

Sully felt his chest tighten, and that *fizz* of magic passing through the air.

It made the hairs stand on end all over his body.

"Very much," he finally got out.

8

ILSNARE PALACE

FLUCKNOR ROAMED the halls with his hand resting on Damon Shriversmyth's shoulder. The house staff had already done the rounds, lighting the torches about the Palace.

The flickering, orange flames caught the stone corridors, turning them a bluish-grey; and scattering reflections in the brass breastplates; the varying swords which hung from the walls.

Flucknor recalled how Lou had rallied against such implements being present in the Palace when he had first taken hold of the Kingdom of Shellacnass; when he had first accepted the Throne.

Lou had claimed that he wanted to rid the Palace halls of all such warmongery.

The fact that Lou hadn't often puzzled Flucknor, although he had finally settled on the explanation that Lou believed that times of war were never far away . . . or, indeed, that they were just around the corner.

As Flucknor passed through the glow of the flickering flames, he felt a slight itch beneath the surface of his skin.

Flucknor knew, from Lou, that this reaction was owing to the ice magic which flowed through his blood. And he had also learned, when Flucknor had described the irritation, that Lou suffered far worse from being near fire.

Since Lou had developed his ice magic powers to a far greater degree as compared with Flucknor, the effect of fire—of *sunlight*— was comparable to hundreds of daggers being constantly thrust into his skin.

When Flucknor had asked Lou about why he insisted on lighting torches in the Throne Room, where Lou's quarters were located, rather than simply being in the darkness, Lou had just muttered something about having to 'walk with weakness'.

To Flucknor, it had sounded more in keeping with the monks' teaching than any sort of code which a mage would follow.

But Flucknor would be first to admit that he knew next to nothing about these things.

Flucknor guided Damon onward, through the deserted, silent corridors. He hadn't realised that it had got so late, and he could already feel Damon's body going frail in his grasp; as if he might collapse at any moment.

Perhaps it would be better for Flucknor to present Damon to Lou in the morning, although Flucknor knew that Lou, as always, would be up most of the night; pacing the Throne Room, his mind on matters which were only known to himself.

Flucknor never dared to pry.

The way he saw it, if Lou wanted to unburden himself with something or other then he would tell it to Flucknor. That case aside, Flucknor was to remain silent.

He supposed this was one of the reasons why Lou had believed Flucknor might make a suitable High Representative . . . and then, he supposed, there was the matter that he was just about the only close friend Lou had.

His only close friend in *Ilsnare*, at least.

Flucknor managed to get Damon all the way up the North-East staircase, and into the room situated beside his own. Once he had got Damon tucked into the already made bed—Ilsnare Palace was constantly on alert for passing, unexpected visitors—Flucknor headed down to the kitchens to see if he might be able to have something prepared for his old father abbot.

Understandably, pickings were poor at that time of night; but Flucknor managed to find a member of the house staff to heat up some of the beef stew which had been prepared earlier on in the evening. And, along with a large, warm loaf of bread—a selection of pears and oranges for dessert—it seemed to be an adequate, nourishing meal for someone in Damon's state.

Flucknor waved off the protests—admittedly quite *laboured* given the time of night—that he should allow a member of the kitchen staff to bring the provisions to Damon's room.

He paced his way through the corridors of the Palace, a silver tray in his hands. The beef stew steamed in its wooden bowl. The pears and oranges teetered on the brink of tumbling off. The loaf of freshly baked bread—originally prepared for breakfast the next morning—rocked back and forth rhythmically; almost pensively.

Just looking at the food stoked a hunger inside Flucknor.

But this was for his father abbot.

For the man who'd so influenced his childhood.

The one who had shown him he *wasn't* a freak . . . and that neither was he a *monster* . . . that he could perform a responsible, *useful* role in the world.

Just like he did now . . .

When Flucknor arrived outside Damon's door, he was surprised to find it was open.

He could've sworn he had shut it behind him when he'd ventured down to the kitchens; so that the draught wouldn't sneak into the bedroom.

Judging from Damon's condition, he wasn't in any sort of state to be catching any of the many sicknesses which constantly floated about Ilsnare.

Flucknor stood in the doorway to Damon's room, aware that he cast a shadow across the floor due to the torchlight in the corridor outside.

He stared into the gloom of the simple—*yet tidy*—quarters.

He could make out a pair of figures in the darkness.

The sound of a muffled voice.

Lou's voice.

Louson Dorf—the King of Shellacnass's—voice.

9

REUNION

A T FIRST Flucknor had no idea what he should do.

He stood in the doorway, staring into the quarters which he had assigned to Damon.

He breathed in the heady, salty smell of the beef stew; the rich, buttery scent of the bread sitting on the tray before him. As he worked to avert his gaze from the scene playing out before his eyes, he found his attention focussed down on the pears and oranges.

They *really did* look succulent.

He supposed that there was some truth to the word about town; about how the King of Shellacnass always got the very finest of the crop—whatever it might be.

Flucknor's attention was only diverted from Damon's provisions when he heard the raspy, familiar voice of Lou.

Lou kept his voice low, and even; at a level just above a whisper. "Flucknor," he said. "Bring the food in, please."

Flucknor hung back for several moments.

He felt another itch pass beneath the surface of his skin; the torchlight again bringing on a reaction from the ice magic in his veins. He put the sensation out of his mind, knowing that he could hardly scratch himself while he continued to grip this silver tray intended for Damon.

He trod into the darkened room, now able to pick out the finer details of the scene.

He saw that Lou sat on the edge of the bed, and that Damon had the sheets drawn up to just beneath his chin. Damon's eyes lolled about their sockets, tracking Flucknor as he approached him with the silver tray. Even in the darkness, Flucknor could see that Damon's complexion was deathly pale.

Might it be that Damon was at death's door?

The thought of it caused a shudder to pass through Flucknor's body.

The fruits, stew and bread which sat on his silver tray quivered.

It was a wonder that nothing fell to the floor.

Flucknor deposited the tray on the bedside table and then turned to leave. He was sure that Damon and Lou had many matters to discuss—*personal matters*—and they would be able to speak much more freely without him there, breathing down their necks.

However, Flucknor had hardly made it two steps to the door before Lou called him back, implored him to take a seat on the edge of Damon's bed.

Again, Flucknor felt a shudder seize control of him.

Although he felt that he had handled the surprise meeting with his former father abbot calmly, and that he had done the right thing in inviting him back to the Palace, he was only now feeling the shockwaves sinking in with him.

That this *really was* his father abbot.

And that he *really had* been pacing the night-time streets of Ilsnare like a hobblesman.

The bed was much squashier than Flucknor's was, and he supposed that, this being a room that was seldom used, the feather mattress was in need of replacing. Perhaps nobody had paid any mind to its maintenance for years.

Lou, certainly, wasn't in the habit of throwing the lush parties of which the previous kings had been so fond. And so there was no need for keeping the extra bedrooms about the Palace in the prim condition to which they'd been accustomed.

Flucknor slipped Damon a sidelong glance, and he met his eye for a second.

He felt a warmth pass through his chest, followed by a tingling —*chilling*—sensation through his blood. He knew that it was his magic responding to him; that it recognised the weight of this reunion; not just between Flucknor and his father abbot, but the one between Lou and Damon.

Even though Flucknor could feel the tears rising up in his eyes, he forced them back down. And he managed to raise a smile to Damon.

As an apprentice, he had sat on many deathbeds of elderly monks, and he had been their dying comfort; holding their hands as he felt the magic dwindle in their veins; their hearts give their final beats.

What mattered now was keeping Damon company.

Damon's eyes swilled in their sockets, and his mouth seemed impossibly small. The way that his skin sagged on his large bones made Flucknor think about how Damon had seemed to waste away in his advancing age.

If only Flucknor had known.

There might've been something he could do.

Seeing as nobody else spoke, Flucknor decided that it must be his turn.

He addressed Damon, his voice shaking a little as he did.

"Father Abbot," Flucknor said, "I thought that you and the other monks had set about rebuilding Ravensbark; that it was flourishing."

Here Flucknor felt his throat constricting and he wondered if he might simply break down in tears . . . how would that be for the stoic image he was attempting to project as the High Representative?

The image which he was *required* to project.

"I . . . I . . ." Flucknor continued, faltering, "I never thought to visit because I didn't think I would be wanted—all the stories; all the *assumptions* . . ." Flucknor thought he would have to strain his mind to remember the exact words, but, as it was, they arrived to the tip of his tongue without any great effort ". . . 'We release those who stray; and return they never shall.' "

The air felt stilted.

Freezing-cold.

When Flucknor turned away so Damon wouldn't see the intense worry which was obviously sketched all over his face, he noticed that the wood-burning stove was empty; that there was no sign of flames within.

"I'm sorry," Flucknor said, rising up off the bed, and padding across the room. "I'll go fetch some kindling."

This time, Flucknor made it halfway down the corridor before Lou called him back.

When Flucknor turned around, it was to observe Lou bringing Damon—his father abbot's—door shut behind him; apparently having left Damon alone to his night-time provisions. Lou's expression remained neutral—*cold*, even.

Flucknor wondered dizzily how Lou could keep himself so distant from a dying man . . . then again, there were facets of the history between Damon and Lou which Flucknor didn't understand; and which he had never felt comfortable asking about.

And which he never would feel comfortable asking about.

Lou approached Flucknor, his eyes fixed onto his.

For several seconds, they stood staring at one another.

And then Lou said, "He has to leave, first thing in the morning."

Flucknor felt every muscle in his body tauten.

He couldn't process the statement, let alone respond.

Before Flucknor had a chance to utter anything, Lou passed by and disappeared off along the corridor.

Apparently headed back to his Throne Room where he would 'walk with weakness' some more.

10

THE GLYPH

TO BEGIN WITH, Sully didn't feel the cold at all.

He remained thoroughly stunned that he was no longer a prisoner in the cave below.

He could hardly believe what had occurred.

The best way he could think to describe it was that one moment he'd been slouched up against the cave wall and the next he had materialised—*somehow*—outside; back on the mounted-up snow above.

The whole scenario seemed like a strange dream—some fantasy which had taken over Sully's brain. He wondered if he would wake up back in the cave below, on the point of starvation, with only his horse's carcass for company.

That would make sense.

That would *follow* logically . . . but, then again, he wasn't down on the plains any longer; he was no longer in a part of the Kingdom strictly under Mortal control.

He was at the very fringes of the Kingdom; the place where magic, and *danger*, lurked around every corner.

He turned back to look at the Glyph; this sprite which'd —*apparently*—freed him.

Sully considered that his previous judgement of the Glyph might've been distorted—taking into account his perilous condition on the cave floor—so he was somewhat surprised to note that the Glyph was pretty much as he had interpreted him earlier.

Grey skin.

Those floppy, somehow velvety ears.

A smooth stomach.

And those large—*large*—eyes.

Sully couldn't help but bring to mind a dog he had had as a child . . . it had escaped only a few weeks after they'd acquired it.

Lying in bed at night, Sully had often wondered what might've happened to that dog; if it had made it to another village, found favour with another family; or if it had simply committed itself to a feral life, out in the wilderness.

As Sully felt himself still reeling from the Glyph's feat of magic —because *magic* was what it was—he heard the Glyph's words within his mind again:

— *You would do well to leave this place, stranger. Darkness and mystery clings to every nook and cranny; and is no place at all for a Mortal. As you have already seen, you can't so much as trust the ground on which you walk.*

Sully lined up a sarcastic reply, but the Glyph anticipated him, apparently hearing what he had in mind to say before he could say it.

— *Very well, stranger. I shall lead you back down and out of the*

Winter's Moan. If we move quickly, we should have you back on the plains before daybreak.

Only then did Sully recall his surroundings, that it was indeed night; and that the only light which illuminated them was from the moon above and the strange, ethereal, lime-green glow which the Glyph emitted.

He glanced back down to the hole in the earth—in the *snow*—beneath his feet.

It was pit-black down there.

Only being up and out of the cave did he realise how fresh the air was; how it no longer stunk of rotting flesh; how the sound of feeding maggots was left behind.

In fact, all that Sully could hear was the distant *whistle* of the wind as it whipped through the mountain passes.

Sully turned back to the Glyph. "I can't leave," he said, "I've come to seek someone out."

"And who should that be, stranger?" the Glyph replied, this time speaking out loud rather than conjuring the words within Sully's mind.

Sully hesitated, afraid to give away his quest despite the fact that this Creature had saved him. Hadn't the Creature itself told him that this was no place for a Mortal? That he couldn't so much as trust the ground he walked upon?

But what else was Sully going to do?

If he examined the facts, realised that he had no horse; that his clothing was *totally* inappropriate for his surroundings; that he had little-to-no food and water; he had to admit to himself that he would never survive alone.

He stared back into the Glyph's wide, rounded eyes. His throat felt dry from lack of water to drink and he prepared to mimic the name which Lou had given him; the mage who Sully had been charged with bringing back to Ilsnare.

"Lumbswich," Sully replied, already worried that he might've pronounced the name wrong . . . although—*somehow*—he couldn't help thinking that the Glyph would know just what he meant from reading his thoughts.

The Glyph stood very still, its head cocked to one side. "What dealings do you have involving Lumbswich?"

Sully shook his head and smiled. "You already know, don't you?"

The Glyph remained stone-faced for a long moment, and then it smiled back at Sully. "I thought it only polite to ask you, stranger." It glanced about, as if paranoid that something might be lurking in the shadows, and—*as far as Sully was concerned*—there might've been. "We had better set off right away; better not to stay too long in this place."

As the Glyph traipsed its way through the snow dunes, apparently not remotely affected by the freezing cold, Sully peered one last time down into the crevice, and then followed the Glyph.

He hoped that this wouldn't prove some fresh folly.

Gods knew, he didn't feel at all positive about *any* of this.

11

UNFORGIVABLE

T HE NEXT MORNING, after the night he had brought Damon in off the streets of Ilsnare, Flucknor stood outside the doors to the Throne Room.

He felt himself shaking all over.

Right down to his toes.

He couldn't remember feeling this afraid since he'd decided to leave Ravensbark behind; when he had been tasked with telling Damon about his decision.

All the same, Flucknor knew that he wouldn't be able to live with himself if he didn't at least *try* to speak to Lou; to make him know how wrong this was.

How they *couldn't* just throw a dying man out onto the street.

Flucknor had felt strange this morning, getting dressed once more in the emerald-green robes of the High Representative. The previous day it had felt something of a novelty to do so; now, though, it was as if the role had become more real . . . as if he had woken up a different person.

Flucknor brought his knuckles up to the oak door. He paused for several moments, feeling his heart bouncing against his throat.

He just needed to do this.

He needed to make himself heard; that was all.

If Flucknor didn't make it known how important this matter was to him, and it came back to haunt their relationship later, Lou wouldn't respect him because he hadn't brought the issue up at the time.

This was the only way.

Flucknor's knock seemed to echo all through the corridor which surrounded him, coming back to him in waves. The echo was almost louder than the response from within.

That he was to enter.

Flucknor took a final moment to smooth the creases from the front of his robes and then he pushed through the oak double doors, and into the Throne Room.

As always, the crimson velvet strips hung down from the walls.

The marble floor matched Flucknor's emerald-green robes.

Up above opened out the beautiful, graceful crystal dome of Ilsnare Palace; the one which could be seen from the plains which surrounded the city; glistening in the golden sunlight.

A searing blue sky beamed down through the glass.

Flucknor recalled when Lou had removed the grey drapes which'd previously concealed the dome; to prevent direct sunlight from flooding in through the roof . . . from afflicting Lou in all those dramatic ways which he had described.

It had been the day that Syre had left the city; when she had been cast into a semi-voluntary exile.

Almost as if Lou wished to punish himself.

Or—as he liked to call it—'to walk with weakness'.

Another crimson, velvet curtain cordoned off the part of the Throne Room which was reserved for Lou's own private quarters.

Flucknor could just make out the tips of the brass poles of Lou's four-poster bed.

He waited patiently, like the good courtier which Lou wished him to be.

Like the respectable High Representative which Lou had made him; the go-to man between the Council of Wisemen and the King.

Lou finally emerged from behind the velvet curtain. He still wore his washed-out, grey-white undershirt which he'd—Flucknor assumed—worn to bed the previous night.

Flucknor assumed that Lou *hadn't* slept in the garment because it was a rare night indeed when Lou slept at all.

His ice magic, as Lou would often tell him, didn't allow him much—if any—rest . . . not these days.

And since Lou had no outlet for his magic, it all simply welled up within his veins; throbbing about his body.

With nowhere to go.

Lou fixed his bleary eyes on Flucknor, and restrained a yawn with the back of his hand. "What is it?" he said, uttering it casually as he trod over to the throne.

When Lou reached the throne, he stood over it for several moments before slumping down on top of the squashy velvet cushion. He propped his chin up with his fist, using the armrest to pivot his elbow.

All at once, Flucknor felt himself stripped of the ability to speak. As so often happened when he arrived to a situation, he found his tongue incapable of communicating with his brain . . . despite how many times he might've drafted—and *redrafted*—his exact words.

Perhaps it was the importance of the matter, just the fact that this was his father abbot who Lou had decided to treat so shabbily, but Flucknor managed to get the words out in the end.

"I want to talk about Damon," Flucknor said. "I want to know why he can't stay."

A slight smile lined Lou's lips. "Because I said so." Lou stifled another yawn with his fist. "Because I'm the *King*."

Flucknor felt his brain probing at this argument; it was so unlike Lou—*this* was all so unlike Lou . . . and yet what Lou said was correct.

He *was* the King.

Flucknor decided to change tack. "Please," he said, "he's dying —don't we owe him a few restful days where he might have enough to eat, enough to drink? It just seems so . . . *heartless* to turn him back out into the street."

Lou pouted. "Spring is coming," he said. "He'll be fine."

Flucknor now felt as though Lou was trying his patience on purpose.

Anger balled within his chest, and he—*almost unconsciously* —bunched his fingers into fists down at his sides. The icy chill of the magic stung his veins now . . . stung him from the *inside.*

But he couldn't stop; he couldn't allow this injustice to pass.

Whatever the reason, Flucknor was determined to beat it down.

"How can you be so *cruel*?" Flucknor finally got out.

Lou flashed his eyes. Then he turned his eyes upward, to the dome in the ceiling, and to the flawless blue sky above. " 'Cruel' ?" Lou replied. " '*Cruel*?' "

Flucknor wasn't going to repeat himself . . . and, anyway, Lou seemed to be doing a good job for him.

Lou breathed in deeply, his shoulders arching back.

Suddenly, he rose up off his throne, took a step toward Flucknor. "Why don't *I* tell you something about cruel, hmm?"

Flucknor felt his chest tighten.

His heart beat a little harder.

Ice pricked his veins.

Lou took yet another step forward.

Flucknor felt a fraught tension enter the air.

It lay against his skin.

He felt it tug on the hairs at the back of his neck.

Lou kept coming forward until he stood only a pace away from Flucknor.

Lou would only have had to reach out and press his hand to Flucknor's forehead to inflict pain on him with his ice magic . . . and Flucknor couldn't help thinking that Lou must be bursting to purge the magic which constantly itched at him from within.

"When I was in training," Lou said, his voice a low snarl. "When all hopes of the Kingdom were placed across my shoulders; do you recall how Damon Shriversmyth treated me?"

Flucknor could remember well.

They had first met at Ravensbark, when Lou had turned up one day.

Flucknor had answered the door to him; and he could still clearly recall the bedraggled image of the young man, only a few years older than he was, standing there, begging to be let in. Although Flucknor thought that he might've twisted the tale in his mind, he was almost certain of *that* detail . . . that Lou had arrived to Ravensbark *begging.*

Lou continued, his tone just as biting as before, "He told me —*begrudgingly*—that I could stay the night; that only because of my friendship with Hilda"—here Flucknor felt his heart leap in his chest because if there was one thing, one person, who was never mentioned about Ilsnare Palace, it was *Hildie* . . . daughter of Ma'reygar—"he would allow me that."

Flucknor stared back into Lou's eyes, and he could see the hatred, true and profound, bubbling away there. He wondered how, after all this time, after all that had gone on later—how Lou had singlehandedly done away with three of the most powerful players in the Kingdom—he could still cling so tightly to a grudge.

But, then again, Flucknor constantly found himself surprised by Lou.

By the things which mattered to him, and which seemed almost *trivial* to Flucknor.

Lou leaned back slightly on his heels now. He glared at Flucknor. "Tell me *why* I shouldn't cast him out into the street, just as he did me?"

Flucknor could only think to repeat what he had before.

"Because he's *dying.*"

Lou shook his head. "Not good enough—some things are *unforgivable.*"

Flucknor decided that there was only one recourse available to him, and that he had no choice but to take it. "If you throw Damon away then I'll leave too."

Lou's gaze smouldered away; his eyes jabbing into Flucknor's.

Although Flucknor hadn't had time to properly consider this threat, it felt the right thing to do.

Just *let* Lou dare him.

A slight smile traced Lou's lips. "You won't do anything of the sort."

Flucknor remained still, staring down the King of Shellacnass.

Still smiling, Lou shook his head. "If you so much as try to leave through the City Gates, I'll have the Royal Guards arrest you immediately—have them place you in the Gaols . . . you'll rot before you ever leave Ilsnare."

Flucknor's whole body became rigid.

Although he had noted Lou's growing cruel tone in their conversation—and throughout the years, as he had grown more and more bitter with his rule—he only now realised that Lou had out-and-out threatened him.

That Lou had put him in his place.

Flucknor could think of nothing else to say.

So he simply bowed his head, as any stranger might do to the King, and then he trod on out of the Throne Room, knowing that he was beaten.

12

FAREWELL

FLUCKNOR WAS SURPRISED to find that Damon was out of bed and dressed when he went by his quarters. When Flucknor looked to the breakfast tray which the house staff had brought in earlier, he saw that the food—fruit, buttered scones and a large jug of orange juice—had only been picked at.

Flucknor looked to Damon who—*somehow*—seemed to read his mind.

"Oh, I can't eat much these days," Damon said. "And certainly not when I have a long journey ahead of me."

"What 'journey' ?" Flucknor said.

Damon gave Flucknor a slight smile, the skin around his mouth and eyes creasing up as he did so. "Please," Damon said, "I know that it's time for me to move on—that I would only be a burden here."

"No," Flucknor replied, stepping toward Damon.

Only when Flucknor stood a few paces away did he risk

reaching out and taking hold of Damon's forearm. He felt the muscles flaccid—*weak*. An old man's atrophied body.

Just like Flucknor's would be one day . . . if he lived as long as Damon.

Damon stared down at where Flucknor gripped his forearm and then he looked back into Flucknor's eyes. "One day you shall understand," Damon said. "One day you shall understand *all* of this."

Flucknor shook his head, and then, feeling a great weight in his heart, he relieved Damon of his grip; allowed his arm to fall back down by his side. "It's not fair," Flucknor said. "You can see that, can't you? How can he hold a grudge for so long, after so many years? And when he hardly understands a *thing* about Ravensbark. You should have heard the threat he made; that he intends to have me locked up if I so much as try to leave Ilsnare!"

Damon held up his palm, apparently not wanting to argue any longer.

Perhaps he was tired of arguing.

He had argued enough in his younger years.

"Before I go," Damon said, "I wanted to tell you about Ravens-bark—I'm sure that you still have questions; about what happened. About why we failed."

Flucknor remained silent.

The last thing he wanted to do was bring up painful topics for Damon—it was clear that he needed his strength for this 'journey' ahead . . .

But Damon, it seemed, would have it no other way.

He started speaking through a sigh, as if the subject itself sent a wave of lethargy through him. "When Ravensbark was first built, it was thought of as being the centre of the magical world; a way for the Four Corners of the Magical Field to retain its calibration; so that mages: fire, ice; light and dark; would know where they stood.

"For many years, it served as this reference point, a means for mages and Magical beings all throughout the land to depend on as a sort of sanctuary from the constant pushes and pulls of the Four Corners; a precarious balance, to be sure, but one which proved to be essential in maintaining the balance of power throughout the world."

Flucknor stared hard at Damon. He thought he could see a slight dampness emerging in his eyes, although it might just as well have been tiredness as emotion.

Damon continued, "When Ma'reygar and his magical army decided to destroy Ravensbark, he also destroyed the only thing which might check the raw power of magic; and it was by this means—*sheer force*—that he hoped to bring down Ilsnare . . . unfortunately for him, as we saw, he hadn't bargained for another harnessing the untapped reservoir of magic and turning it not just against him but against Auch'ray and his adversary Herimyre."

Flucknor was in no hurry for Damon to leave. He hadn't yet decided how he might handle this situation. If he might just decide to leave Lou to his moping and go elsewhere; where he might be of better use. He lifted his head to reply. "And when you returned to rebuild Ravensbark, to recreate the sanctuary from before?"

"Ravensbark, as it turns out, was precariously balanced. And, as such, when we—*the monks*—returned to the spot where Ravensbark once resided, we found soon enough that it was simply impossible to replicate what we once had."

"You gave up?" Flucknor replied, unable to stop himself raising his eyebrows to this statement . . . he had never met anybody as singularly minded as Damon Shriversmyth—*his father abbot*—in the entirety of his life.

Damon gave a solemn nod. "I suppose you could put it that way. As it turned out, the recreation of Ravensbark was beyond any of our abilities as monks. Although it is not well known who first founded the monastery, whoever it was must've had an extremely comprehensive understanding of not just magic but of Shellacnass. An understanding which we lacked."

"But I don't understand," Flucknor went on, "you returned to the same spot; you set about rebuilding brick by brick . . . why wouldn't you be successful?"

Damon shook his head. "Magical wars are powerful things— and the destruction of such a sacred place as Ravensbark does not go unnoticed by the Magical Fields. It leaves a scar upon the land. My theory as to why we could no longer rebuild Ravensbark on the same spot was because the Magical Fields had shifted . . . something *intangible* had changed . . . something we—*as humble monks*—had no chance of being able to influence."

Flucknor still felt it somewhat mind-blowing that there were certain aspects of the world—*especially magic*—which Damon hadn't yet mastered the knowledge of.

Back when Flucknor had been an apprentice, growing up within the stone walls of Ravensbark, he had always seen Damon as a never-ceasing fountain of knowledge.

Even now, years later, it was greatly surprising for him to find this image he'd built up in his childhood shattered.

"What about the other monks?" Flucknor said, following up.

Damon shrugged and then shook his head. "We all sort of drifted apart—all of us going our separate ways."

Flucknor wondered how many of them had become hobblesmen like Damon—directionless, moving from place to place without any destination in mind.

Perhaps if Flucknor had remained with the monks the same fate would've befallen *him*.

Who was to say?

Damon gave Flucknor a broad smile and then reached out and clapped him on the shoulder. "Well," he said, "I suppose you'd better show me to the door, don't you think?"

As Flucknor took Damon down through the Palace, he felt the same anger brewing within him, about how Lou was throwing Damon out into the street.

For all that Damon might've offended Lou in the past, it seemed a new kind of heartlessness to commit this act on this elderly man; this *weak* man.

Only when Flucknor had brought Damon to the Palace Gates, and with the Royal Guards standing upright, looking on as they held their spears pointed up to the sky, did Flucknor think to ask the question which'd bothered him for so long.

Not just since he had met with Damon but all the years since he had left the monks behind.

Flucknor looked to Damon, their eyes meeting for what Flucknor knew would be the final time. "What do you think I should do? What do you think I *am*?"

Damon smiled slightly in reply, and then he looked out beyond the Palace Walls, to the Crystal City beyond; the glass rooftops just beginning to catch the golden sunrise.

"Well, I think the only one who can answer that is yourself."

"What I mean," Flucknor continued, trying to get what he wanted to say right in his brain, "is that I've felt this urge to indulge my ice magic; to learn more about it." He paused for a long moment. "But I feel that certain things—certain *people*—are holding me back; are trying to keep me from attaining whatever I might be able to *attain*."

Damon smiled wider, apparently understanding just which 'people' Flucknor was referring to.

"I suppose what I want to ask is if I should explore that direction—if I should go down the same path as Louson, explore becoming an ice mage."

Here Damon's smile lessened slightly. "Nobody can go down the same path as anybody else—everybody forges their *own* path."

Flucknor allowed himself to absorb this reply for several seconds, and then, acting on impulse, he leaned forward and grabbed hold of Damon—his *father abbot*.

He hugged him tightly to his chest and could think of nothing except for the fact that he'd never see him again.

It was then that Flucknor heard the muttered words; so quiet that he might have equally imagined Damon had said nothing at all.

"*Walk in the light.*"

When Flucknor finally released Damon, they said nothing to one another.

Damon simply turned his back to him and trod off out of the Palace Gates; his hobblesman's cloak tight about his body. And his face obscured by the hood.

Another orphaned man.

Might Flucknor turn out the same?

13

LONG DARK NIGHT

S ULLY paused on the track.

He leaned all his weight against the iced-over rock face.

He brought his arms up to his chest and then rubbed them together; hoping to instil some sort of warmth into his blood.

His teeth chattered so hard that he could barely hear himself think . . . although—on reflection—he supposed this something of a bonus considering that the Glyph was capable of reading his thoughts.

He glanced about.

The moonlight dimly lit up the landscape.

Mountain tops glazed with snow and ice.

Ominous dark clouds lolling about on the horizon.

A storm was the very last thing Sully needed.

A storm was all it would take to finish him off.

It was easy for him to spot the Glyph, the lime-green light illuminating it against the pure, white snow piled up on the ground.

Apparently sensing that Sully had halted his advance, the Glyph turned and looked over its shoulder at him. It frowned. "Hurry up!" the Glyph said. "We will not make it there at this rate —you will *freeze* to death first!"

Sully couldn't help but feel that what the Glyph said was correct; and yet he was beginning to feel the creeping realisation that he couldn't care less.

What would it matter if he froze into a block of ice?

Perhaps it would go some way to showing Lou how he had overestimated him . . . not to mention teach him a lesson about using long-suffering friends as errand boys.

But then Sully thought about the location of the Webbing Armoury; about how he—*and Rut*—were the only ones in the world who held the key to its location.

If Sully died here—if he *froze* to death—then the Webbing Armoury might prove to be impossible for the next generations to find.

. . . And with a certain sense of cynicism, Sully couldn't help but wonder if that was what Lou intended—if it was his desire to hide the Webbing Armoury from the world by doing away with its pair of gatekeepers; by doing away with himself and Rut.

As Sully pushed himself back off the rock face, he couldn't help wondering if Rut had found himself in a similarly perilous dilemma . . .

Would it make him feel better to think that his rotund companion, Rut, was braced in some life-death struggle?

Hardly.

On reflection, Sully would've liked nothing more than for the two of them to be tucked up in some cosy tavern somewhere—*a log-fire blazing away*—both of them with a pint of honey ale to hand; their cheeks reddened from the effects of the fermented beverage.

But, as Sully felt another biting—*cutting*—wind soar through the pass and run through the thin material of his tunic, this hypothetic tavern seemed a Very Long Way Off Indeed.

Sully glanced back up at the Glyph, seeing the insistent lime-green glow which accompanied his odd, squat, grey-skinned body. He wondered how long it would be before sunrise.

And, more to the point, how long it would be before he could feel warm again.

14

REFLECTION

FLUCKNOR'S HEART seemed to weigh down his whole body as he plodded through the Palace corridors. He was still wearing his emerald-green robes associated with his role as the High Representative, but he hadn't yet been summoned by Lou to deliver a message to the Council of Wisemen.

Quite simply put, there was nothing for Flucknor to do except wait.

He wondered if his weakness had to do with skipping breakfast. He hadn't been able to eat with the knowledge that Damon—his former father abbot—would be alone and out on the road.

Or was it because Flucknor knew that he was trapped?

That following Damon simply wasn't an option?

Although Flucknor had never intended to leave Lou's side, he had always held the deep belief that—if he so wished—he could leave the Crystal City at any time of his choosing.

Now, though, he realised that his freedom—that his *free will*—

had been nothing but a façade; perhaps even an intended delusion on Lou's part . . . hoping to keep Flucknor happy as if he was some rat in a cage with a hunk of cheese being dangled on a string just above his head . . . always just *slightly* out of reach.

Never truly attainable.

And yet, Flucknor only had himself to blame; he had been the one who had chosen to leave Damon and the monks all those years back. He had believed that his future lay at Lou's side; that Lou might grow to depend on him.

But, in truth, Flucknor was nothing more than a pawn.

Just another Mortal with a touch of magical blood to prop up Lou's crumbling kingdom.

The Crystal Kingdom, indeed . . . just what was so *grand* about it now?

Following some invisible path laid out by his subconscious, Flucknor eventually found himself standing back in Damon's room; in the room which he had brought Damon to the night before.

He saw that the silver tray, with the uneaten remnants of Damon's breakfast, still remained on the bedside table.

How Damon could survive on so little sustenance was a source of great thought for Flucknor as Flucknor himself had never had to truly suffer . . .

Ever since his parents had handed him over to the Ravensbark monks, he had been looked after.

He had never missed so much as a meal.

How well Lou had known him to call his bluff; to know that Flucknor most likely wouldn't survive *a week* on the measly rations served in the Palace Gaols!

Of course, there was no question of Flucknor escaping the

Crystal City; of him leaving Lou alone, to suffer the consequences of whatever grumbling nature had seized him.

And which had held him all these years.

Flucknor found himself staring down at the silver tray, studying the reflection of the little sunlight which dribbled on in through the window shutters in its surface.

And then, as if some invisible elbow nudged him in the ribs, he found himself staring long and hard at the yellowed piece of parchment. Folded in half and tucked neatly underneath the tray.

Flucknor glanced back to the doorway, as if Lou might be tracking his every move, as if Lou's suspicions of an impending betrayal from the one who had been most loyal to him throughout these years had come to obsessive efforts.

But nobody was there.

Nobody in the doorway, or out in the corridor, as far as Flucknor could tell.

Flucknor slipped the note out from beneath the tray, unfolded it and then read the scrawled, black-inked handwriting within:

Dear Fluck,

I am writing to you to let you know that I'm well; and that you're not to worry about me. I bumped into Damon Shriversmyth in one of the Northern Villages. Don't worry! I'm very much sticking to the terms of my exile and keeping my nose clean as well as I can manage, leaving Ilsnare behind. I decided to give Damon this note since he intended to pass by Ilsnare on his way to, well, wherever it is he intends to go . . .

I plan on continuing north; and then up and out of the Kingdom.

*That will put a strain on the method of correspondence which
we've developed.*

Flucknor surfaced from the letter for a moment.

He cast his mind back to the knot in the tree stump—just
outside the City Walls—where he would pass by and check for
notes from Syre . . .

Did this mean that they were finished with that now?

That this could be the last note he would receive from her
until . . . well, who knew when?

He went on reading:

*I wouldn't expect to hear anything more from me in the near
future.*

Just to read that line felt like an icicle had been jabbed directly
into his heart.

It was one thing for Lou to prohibit him from so much as
venturing out through the City Walls, but it was something altogether to be entirely cut off from the outside world.

From the woman he loved.

Perhaps forever . . .

*I know that this will not be an easy note for you to receive, but,
well, I'm sure that we both understand the nature of the world;
about how things have panned out. Damon has told me about
Ravensbark, but I shall leave that for him to explain when he
sees you in the flesh. He tells me that you're to trust in Louson,
whatever happens, and that you're to stay by his side. It's now
more important than ever that Lou has your protection.*

Flucknor felt his hands, apart from himself, grip the piece of parchment so tightly that a tear developed near the base of the page.

But he forced himself to read right to the end:

Already I've seen and learned so much on my travels. I feel as though I've grown as a person—and now I hope to grow myself as a mage. To be someone who not only you and Lou can look up to, but who the entire Kingdom of Shellacnass can be proud of.

Someone who can control.

My love,

Syre

Thoughts whizzed through Flucknor's mind as he considered the note.

All that stuff about 'control' . . . that was all he had ever over-heard of the conversations between Syre and Lou; about the *need* for her to 'control' her magic better . . .

If only Flucknor had ventured as far on his own quest of magical discovery that he might have some working comprehension of just what the importance of 'control' might entail.

But, it seemed, that was just another in the long string of secrets which Lou had kept from him.

Was it so that Lou might always be superior?

So that Flucknor might never get ideas that he could challenge the King; that Flucknor one day might come close to competing with Louson Dorf, the Fearsome Ice Mage?

Flucknor could feel his ice magic itching through his veins and he knew—*deep within*—there was the desire to know more. The *need* to know more. And yet he knew that, in Ilsnare—in this damn *Palace!*—he had learned all that he ever could about himself; and about the world.

But what choice did he have now?

What choice did Lou offer him?

. . . None expect to be a mediocrity; to be nothing more than a messenger boy diligently keeping open a line of dialogue between the Council of Wisemen and the King.

Was that all the future held for him?

Flucknor crumpled the parchment into a ball.

For a long while he clung tight to it and then he turned to look at the open fire; the one which he had lit the night before for Damon.

A few crackling embers continued to glow there.

Acting on impulse, he tossed the parchment into the fireplace; and he watched on as, slowly, gradually, the flames massaged their way up the tightly packed ball.

When he heard the voice in the doorway; the voice of a member of the house staff enquiring as to whether she could take the silver breakfast tray, he felt every muscle in his body draw rigid . . . as if it might be some evil-hearted mage ready to kill him where he stood.

He held himself together, turned to the member of the house staff, and gave a subtle nod that he wasn't sure would be perceptible.

As the member of the house staff set about gathering up Damon's breakfast tray, Flucknor stood over the fireplace, staring into the flames; watching the note—the *final* note from Syre— burn down into ashes.

That was all she was to him.

All *anyone* was to him now.

Just ashes.

15

AN UNFORTUNATE TRUTH

E VEN with the mid-afternoon sun on his back, Sully's entire body still felt as if it had been rendered a block of ice . . . and one which had little chance of thawing given the freezing temperature of the air.

The Glyph, though, seemed completely unaffected by the temperature, or—indeed—by the layer-upon-layer of snow which frosted the ground beneath their feet.

It had been over a week now since the Glyph had aided Sully in his escape from the cave . . . or had it been so much as *two* weeks?

Sully had lost track of time.

One thing, though, was for certain.

If Sully hadn't come across the Glyph—or, perhaps more accurately, if the Glyph hadn't come across *him*—then he would've been nothing but a particularly interesting block of ice.

Up ahead, the Glyph paused. Its lime-green glow shone all

around, setting the crystal-white snow in a strangely ethereal light. It glanced about itself then turned its attention back to Sully, wearing a slight smile.

Once Sully was close enough so that the Glyph could make its voice heard, it spoke.

The Glyph had apparently, rightly, throughout their time travelling together, clicked that Sully found hearing its voice within the realms of his own skull uncomfortable.

"Just ahead here, we are almost there."

Sully could hardly believe the Glyph—it seemed too good to be true.

Even despite the conditions having nearly frozen him solid, and the rampant hunger and thirst which had afflicted him throughout the day; he couldn't help but feel his spirits lightening measurably.

Maybe there *was* some hope after all.

The Glyph led Sully through a path in the snow, about a piece of the rock face which stuck out and—*unpleasantly*, for Sully—made the long drop to the snow-encrusted valley below even more likely.

Sully was quite surprised, given the clumsiness which'd accompanied him throughout this journey so far coupled with his hunger and thirst, that he didn't totter over the edge.

Maybe the Glyph was working some sort of magic to keep Sully well balanced.

That must be it.

When they did turn the corner, Sully was surprised to see—up here, in the Winter's Moan; in the middle of nowhere—that there was a round-topped hut, apparently weaved out of nothing but leaves and twigs and mud; its rooftop coated in snow.

And although no light emanated from within—no sign of a fire—Sully couldn't help but feel himself getting his hopes up.

That this Glyph had steered him right all along.

Over the past few weeks of their travels, the Glyph had been sure to keep Sully well-watered and well-fed; always seeming to find him something to eat before the sun set on the horizon.

As each day passed by, Sully realised that he was becoming more and more dependent on the Glyph . . . he couldn't quite wrap his head around what might become of him if the Glyph—*one evening*—decided not to bother with the food or water; or, worse still, decided to simply leave him here, in the middle of nowhere.

What had Sully done to deserve such caring attention from this Creature?

Sully put those ponderings to one side for the time being and focussed on the hut ahead. He looked to the Glyph and said, "Is this it—is this where Lumbswich lives?"

The Glyph's round eyes grew rounder still. Its lips became slightly pert. "Well, it would be something of a disappointment if it turned out *not* to be . . ."

Sully had grown accustomed to the Glyph's slightly acerbic wit throughout their time together, and he had learned not to take the comments as a personal attack on his own intelligence; that the Glyph was, more than likely, fatigued by the company of a Mortal.

Oftentimes, Sully had noted this same kind of attitude in other Magical beings; even in Lou. As if a *mere Mortal* like Sully, or Rut, for that matter, hadn't the slightest inkling of the true image of the world simply because there was no form of magic flowing through their veins.

Sully, with the Glyph dropping back to walk beside him, approached the hut half-buried in the snow. He hadn't much of a briefing on what sort of etiquette he should exercise. Since there didn't seem to be anywhere to knock, Sully decided that the best he could do to announce his presence was to call out.

And so he did.

The Glyph seemed to take exception to this action, although it was true to say that it didn't propose any sort of alternative.

The two of them stood outside the snow-buried hut, awaiting a response.

Finally, when a response wasn't forthcoming, the Glyph turned to Sully, that same smile smeared all over its lips; and its odd lime-green light bringing out the darkened, subtle contours of its face. "Perhaps we should take a look inside?" the Glyph said.

Sully held himself still.

Although he might not know much about mages, he knew enough that one of the best pre-emptive defences which a Mortal could practise was politeness.

And sticking his nose in somewhere it didn't belong certainly *didn't* follow that particular line.

"Can't you . . ." Sully began, and then paused.

He shook his hand at the hut as if to imply conjuring . . . but it didn't seem the Glyph followed him.

He decided to put his desires into words.

"You know, *do* some magic?" Sully added, finally.

The Glyph stood stock-still, staring at the hut, apparently as reluctant to make the first move as Sully.

Sully supposed that in the Winter's Moan a policy of not being the one to take the first step was congruent with life expectancy.

The Glyph turned its attention to the hut. Its eyelids drooped down. Only the slits of its eyes showed. For several seconds it stood there and stared.

Finally, it turned its attention back to Sully. "I can sense magic . . . but it's weak—*very weak*."

Sully felt his heart dip in his chest.

It would be just his luck to have come all this way—all this way out to this forsaken *place*—only to find that he had been given the wrong directions.

He turned back to the Glyph. "What do you think?" he said. "Should we go back?"

The Glyph eyed him closely. "You haven't been on many quests —have you?"

In fact, as the case was, Sully had been on *plenty* of quests . . . and, as Royal Protector of the Plains, there had been many times when he had learned it was time for him to give up whatever it was he was chasing.

And this seemed just like one of those situations.

A *cut-your-losses* type of situation.

"Come on," Sully said, decided now, "let's take a look inside."

Sully noted, as he approached the hut, how the Glyph kept itself well back; again seeming to follow that unwritten rule of the Winter's Moan . . .

When Sully finally got to the opening of the hut, he was surprised to find that there was nothing blocking it; not even so much as a piece of material dangling down.

Within, he could make out the gloom.

Nothing but gloom.

It was right then, with his palms laid firmly flat on his kneecaps that Sully suddenly felt an *overwhelming* stench emanate from within.

He turned his head away, but the stink was almost powerful

enough to knock him right over; to cause him to fall into the snow dune beneath his feet.

Somehow he managed to stay standing.

Apparently sensing that there wasn't any immediate *physical* danger, the Glyph soon arrived at Sully's side. "What?" it said. "What *is* it?"

Sully felt the bile bite at the back of his throat.

He shook his head, trying to rid himself of the foul odour.

But it felt as if he never quite would.

The Glyph ventured into the hut, seemingly unperturbed by the unholy smell. Once it was some way inside, it called back to Sully. "Dead," it said.

Even through the tears streaming from his eyes, Sully managed to lift his head up and reply.

"What?"

"Lumbswich," the Glyph repeated. "He's *dead.*"

16

THE HIGH TRAITOR

I N THE WEEKS which followed Damon's departure, Flucknor did his best in his day-to-day role as High Representative.

He also made a concerted effort to remain distant whenever Lou called on him; for him to deliver this or that message to the Council of Wisemen at the Galleries of Justice.

Strangely, as time went on, Flucknor found himself developing a better and better rapport with the Council of Wisemen. And he couldn't quite help but chuckle along with the subtle jokes the Council of Wisemen often made at Lou's expense—at the *King's* expense . . . at how the King held nothing but a ceremonial role in Shellacnass while the Council, in truth, held the *real* power.

He found himself, too, becoming more convinced by the arguments of the Council; the ones which followed the line preaching the continuation of the status quo . . . for Magical beings—*Creatures among them*—to be denied the same rights as Mortals.

As they—*themselves*—argued, it was a fact that magic was

already well integrated throughout the whole of the Kingdom and, as such, there was little benefit to be found from introducing any new, state-wide laws to guarantee protections for Magical beings.

Wouldn't Magical beings—willing to work their way through Mortal systems—indeed have a distinct advantage in concealing the magic which ran through their veins; in their being able to live in these Mortal realms with such great power held within them unseen?

It made Flucknor think back to what Brotsboore had told him when he had refused him entry to the Creatures' meeting. That the Creatures were tired of being forced to hide their true forms in Mortal society . . . but what sort of a kingdom would Shellacnass be if Creatures were afforded freedoms; if magic was made commonplace?

How would Mortals be able to compete with magic?

It might be that any decision to afford Creatures rights would only be at the expense of Mortals being able to live out productive, contented lives in what was—*first and foremost*—a Mortal kingdom.

Another idea which Flucknor had floated before the Council, and had been surprised to not have shot down before it had a chance to gestate, was the creation of a parallel kingdom: a place where Creatures could go and live out their lives without the need to hide themselves. New societies where they could practise magic openly and without fear of reproach . . .

Those who couldn't bear playing the Mortal games—who couldn't bear *living a lie*—could go and live there; and be happy.

More and more, Flucknor felt himself influenced by the Council of Wisemen; and more than once he arrived in the Throne Room to speak with Lou about something or other only to find Lou indifferent to whatever topic it was that they discussed.

Soon enough, Flucknor was able to predict Lou's indifference to such an extent that he could confidently speak on behalf of the King.

And that was truly a *great* power, indeed.

One night, Flucknor ventured home from the Galleries of Justice—as always shirking the offer of a horse-drawn carriage back to the Palace—always wanting to walk among the city as it packed up for the day.

He wore his sable overcoat over the top of his emerald-green robes, wanting to keep something of a low profile . . . previous High Representatives had had no such concerns; often very much enjoying showing off their exclusive privilege to the citizens of Ilsnare as if they might be an example for the wretched to follow, or something like that . . . but Flucknor was more cautious.

He didn't want to rile anybody unnecessarily.

Didn't want to make *enemies* unnecessarily.

Perhaps he was cut out to be a politician after all.

While Flucknor paced his way along the Crystal Causeway, he breathed in the heady stench of the fish that had been dumped into the River Ils; left to drift on out through the city's sewage systems and eventually down onto the plains. He pictured in his mind the banks outside the City Walls where hobblesmen and peasants would gather to scoop up what goodness they might be able to find in the dirty water from the Crystal City.

Often he wondered if there might be something done for the hobblesmen and peasants; if some permanent solution might be reached.

They were not permitted access to the Crystal City, of course;

the Royal Guards would see to that, stopping them at the gates. That was one of the reasons why crime was kept so low within the City Walls, and it was a reputation—a *fact*—which Flucknor intended to keep up for the duration of his role as High Representative.

Living like a scavenger was no life at all.

Even back in the village where he had grown up—back in Dweldwock, where people had been poor—everyone, without exception, had learned a trade.

Earned their living.

It was when Flucknor started down his regular route, the snaking, labyrinthine back lane which led up to the Palace Gates, that he could sense somebody following him.

He reached into his cloak, feeling for his dagger.

It would be just his luck that he would have a run-in with a mugger . . . but the mugger wouldn't be expecting Flucknor to be ready and waiting—with a *blade* in hand.

Feeling his heart beating against his ribs in anticipation, Flucknor kept up his progress along the cobblestones, keeping his head tilted downward so he could get a better look at his pursuer.

His pursuer wore a cloak, just like him—just like the *majority* of the citizens of Ilsnare.

Flucknor was confident of beating his pursuer for pace.

That he would reach the Palace Walls, and the relative safety of the Royal Guards posted all along the ramparts, before the pursuer caught up to him.

They would get a *real* shock when they saw who he was.

When they realised what power he wielded throughout the city.

And, more than likely, they would regret their actions until the day they died . . .

Flucknor turned his attention to the lane ahead—the neat cobblestones.

And then he saw another of the cloaked figures.

Another—*still*—emerging behind the first one.

He glanced back over his shoulder again, this time taking no efforts to be subtle.

There were three cloaked figures trailing him now.

There would be no way out of this . . . *unless* . . .

He broke into a run.

At the same time, he slipped his dagger from its sheath.

He held it down at his thigh as he bounded toward the pair of cloaked figures boxing him into the tiny lane. As he got closer to them, he watched them form a barrier—clearly attempting to stop him getting past.

Without thinking, he brought the dagger up and swung it wildly, hoping that he might be able to catch one of them in the face.

The blade made contact with flesh.

A *groan* sounded in his ear.

Right in his ear.

Before he could shoulder barge the remaining cloaked figure —blocking his path—he felt invisible hands seize him.

About his throat.

Tighten their grasp about his chest.

Slowly—*gradually*—he sensed his feet leaving the ground.

The soles of his boots leaving the cobblestones below.

At first, he was certain that it was his own magic; that he'd somehow managed to tap into some sort of survival mechanism; and that he was going to free himself from this perilous encounter.

And it was with that thought on his mind that he felt his entire body being hurled unceremoniously downward—*hard* against the cobblestones.

Then the world went black.

17

CAPTURED

THE FIRST THING which struck Flucknor was the smell.

The smell of smoke.

It covered his nostrils.

Gagged his mouth.

He could feel the tickle of ash at the back of his throat, creeping its way down into his lungs.

He heard crackling flames working away at logs in a fireplace nearby.

When he finally opened his eyes, his vision was bleary.

He could only make out the most basic of shapes.

A figure. Nearby.

Several figures.

The furniture—armchairs, and tables . . . then the stone floor.

It all swayed as he felt a wave of giddiness descend over his thoughts.

He wondered if he would black out again.

If the world would leave him once more.

But then he fastened his attention onto the emerald-green robe—*the High Representative's robe*—which hung from a hook across the room.

Not much more than a blur.

He realised that he was only in his underclothes.

What had happened before—*where he had been when he'd been attacked*—slowly returned.

He had risen up in the air.

Floated above the ground . . . only to be brought *crashing* back down.

He wondered if that sensation—that feeling of *flying*—was how Syre felt whenever she transformed into a crow.

What Flucknor wouldn't do for the ability to transform himself into an animal—*any animal*—right at this moment.

Even as a mouse he might have the hope of escape.

He straightened out his perception enough to realise that he was sitting on a chair—a *hard-backed, wooden* chair.

His wrists had been bound behind his back. His ankles, too, had been tied to the chair legs.

He supposed that if he had tried to force his weight upward, he might've been able to hop the chair along the stone floor. But what would that have achieved? It only would've notified his captors that he was awake; that he had regained his

. . .

— *We can hear your thoughts, Flucknor.*

Flucknor's heart bounced up to the back of his mouth.

He swallowed hard, feeling the dry, flaky ash smothering his tongue.

He had heard that voice . . . *within* his own mind . . . and before he quite got a handle on that concept, he heard words enter his skull once again:

— *Don't worry, we didn't do any permanent damage. But, as you shall realise with the coming time, it was a necessary evil; capturing you like that.* Kidnapping *you.*

Flucknor tried to shrug his shoulders, and found that his muscles were stiff; almost unmoving. He blinked several times, trying to free the bleariness from his eyes.

As if to confirm that the voice had control of Flucknor's brain; that it could not only input words into his mind, but read his thoughts, it added:

— *We administered a potion, and its effects will wear off in a matter of hours. Your vision shall return to its normal state. But it was important, I hope you will see later, that you understand that we hold you in absolute dominion; that whenever we wish to snatch you—whether that be on the streets of the city; or in your bed—then we shall do so.*

Is that clear?

Flucknor had no idea what to say by way of response.

He was still trying to make sense of the bleary room before him.

When he attempted to speak aloud, he felt as if invisible fingers held down his tongue.

He realised he must reply to the voice within his mind:

— *Yes.*

The next time the voice appeared within his mind, he somehow recognised the tone, the timbre of the words; and he realised that it was Brotsboore.

What the voice said next only served to confirm this:

— *Much depends on you, Flucknor; we depend on you, brother. Do not take your casting-out personally; those who cast out others often do so for a reason much greater than the individual.*

And you, Flucknor, have so much capacity for good; a way of the light about you . . . and it would be a great shame for it to come to waste; for us to have to destroy you.

But, if needs must . . .

It was then that Flucknor felt himself fading again—felt his *mind* fading again.

The final effect was just as swift as snuffing out a candle with a clasped palm.

Poof . . . and the flame was gone.

Darkness returned.

18

AT JOURNEY'S END

S ULLY FELT the gentle warmth of the flames rising up from
the campfire.

The heat reflected off the stone walls which surrounded him.

He breathed in the scent of soil and thought back to the
verdant plains which he had left behind.

As Royal Protector of the Plains, Sully had been granted his
own cottage—not a large abode, by his request; he had never been
one to aspire to live in mansions or palaces, or the like. All he
wished for was a little patch of dirt to call his own and a roof over
his head.

The four walls of his cottage were just a bonus.

His stomach felt filled with the rabbit the Glyph had caught
and then promptly skinned and roasted over the naked flames.

The first time that Sully had really felt the satisfaction of a
good meal since he had left home.

In fact, he thought he could get used to the Glyph's cooking.

Adjusting his weight on the log where he sat, Sully turned to the cave mouth.

The darkness had closed in several hours ago and—after having eaten his own, suspiciously meagre, portion of rabbit—the Glyph had ventured back out again. To do what, Sully really had no idea, and he supposed it was no one but the Glyph's business what he *did* do.

Not knowing where to go next, what he should *do* after finding the ice mage Lumbswich dead in his home—due to old age, as the Glyph had claimed—Sully had taken the executive decision to remain in close proximity to Lumbswich's home for the next few days.

For what reason, he wasn't entirely sure.

Perhaps it was the prospect of returning to Ilsnare Palace empty-handed; after Lou had given him such a clear task.

Sully had never enjoyed letting people down—in fact, he had often done everything within his power to prevent it from happening.

This time, though, there seemed no solution.

Lumbswich was *dead.*

Sully and the Glyph had spent a great deal of time and energy digging out a grave for the ice mage; somewhere for him to be laid to rest. It had seemed the right thing to do.

They had marked his grave with a simple stone from the rock face.

Tomorrow, Sully had decided, he would leave this place behind; and he would start on his journey back to Ilsnare to report on what had occurred. And, as he craned his neck to look out through the cave opening once more, he hoped that the Glyph would return to guide him back to the plains . . . Sully *really* didn't fancy walking back all the way on his own. Without sufficient guidance, he was convinced that he would end up taking a tumble down yet another crevice in the earth; hidden by the piled-up snow.

As Sully sat still, listening to his own breathing, he realised he could hear footsteps.

Outside the cave.

He held himself still.

Listened to his heartbeat.

And then he turned his attention to the footsteps.

The gentle, percussive, persistent:

Scrunch. Scrunch. Scrunch.

A deer?

A bear?

A *wolf*?

He supposed that it could really be any sort of animal.

His chest tightened and he found that he suddenly couldn't keep himself still.

He rose up off the log and—taking extreme care—trod over to the cave mouth.

He peered out at the area surrounding—*out into the darkness*—and could, unsurprisingly, see *nothing*.

He breathed in deeply, taking the frosty, night-time air into his lungs.

When he exhaled, his breath formed a cloud.

The sound of footsteps had ceased now . . . but that didn't mean the danger had passed.

Quite the opposite.

Sully felt that same static crackle pass through the air when he turned his head to inspect the trees on the other side of the clearing.

There was a flash of bright, silver light.

Light which—Sully knew—could only indicate a *hex*.

Thinking fast, he ducked.

Rocks crumbled then fell as dust upon his head.

He tried to regain his balance in his crouched position, but he failed.

He fell over, sprawling onto his back.

As he quickly moved his limbs, hoping to find his feet once again—so that he might make *some* attempt at escape—he heard the voice of his aggressor sound above him.

"Move and you die."

Sully quickly made the decision to lie still.

To do *nothing* in fact.

He waited to see if another hex would skitter through the air, directed at his head . . . but it never came.

He glued his eyes to the cave mouth, waiting to see who might walk through the opening. And, clad in a sable cape, with the hood drawn down to her shoulders—hands gripping the air before her and neon-blue strands of ice magic clinging to her fingertips—Sully saw just who it was.

"Syre?" he just about got out.

19

PARANOIA IN THE CRYSTAL CITY

EVERY MORNING when Flucknor woke up he could feel his mind reeling with the details of his kidnap; of how he'd been minding his own business, walking home from the Galleries of Justice, when he'd been snatched.

Even as he dressed himself in his emerald-green robes, the clothing which marked him out as the High Representative, he felt his hands shaking; as if those who had snatched him—the Horrox —might be lurking behind his bedroom drapes.

Just as they had threatened.

That they could get him anywhere.

Anytime.

Flucknor knew why they had done it—they had even explained it to him.

Although he had been cast out by their organisation, told in no uncertain terms by Brotsboore that he was no longer welcome at the meetings owing to his day job as High Representative, he knew that they would continue to watch him.

That they heard what he said to the Council of Wisemen.

It would be naïve to think that the Horrox didn't have eyes and ears spread throughout the whole of Ilsnare. Just as the Council of Wisemen had discussed over the past few weeks, if a Creature really wanted success for themselves in this Mortal kingdom then they could easily achieve it . . . if they were subtle about using their powers.

Creatures who didn't have transformative capabilities, of course, would find it much harder going. If they couldn't pass for Mortal at the City Gates, they wouldn't be allowed into Ilsnare to begin with.

Casting his mind back to those who had kidnapped him, he was convinced that the Creatures had caught wind—disapproved of—his proposal for another kingdom; one in which magic would be set free; where there would be none of the restrictions common within the Mortal world.

It was obvious that Brotsboore and the others wanted no compromise; they wanted only freedom and equality . . . and among Mortals.

Several times, Flucknor had been on the cusp of telling Lou what had happened to him.

He knew that if he did, Lou would instantly send out a group of Royal Guards to arrest the offenders; and no matter how well the Horrox—Brotsboore and the rest—hid themselves, even in Mortal bodies, they would be discovered and taken to the Gaols.

But Flucknor had no intention of doing that.

In fact, he was secretly glad that they *had* snatched him off the street.

His new role had had a much more subtle effect on him than he might've imagined; gently pushing him into being someone who he wasn't.

Or someone he *believed* he wasn't.

He thought back to his thoughts on the peasants, on the hobblesmen fishing leftovers out of the Ils as it flowed beneath the City Walls and out onto the plains.

Did he have any right to judge them?

He supposed that he had just about as much right to judge them as they had the right to judge *him*.

One morning, just after Flucknor had polished off a breakfast of scrambled eggs and ham, a member of the house staff announced that he had been summoned by the King.

Wiping his lips with a silk napkin, he felt that same sense of dread deep in his gut.

Before he had always been glad to share Lou's company.

Now, though, it all seemed quite different.

Now that Lou had made the threat so openly—announcing that Flucknor wouldn't be allowed to leave the city unless Lou *personally* willed it—their relationship had become understandably strained.

Sometimes Flucknor wondered if Lou had longed for their relationship to be like this ever since they had met. If Flucknor had learned one thing about Lou over the years it was that he didn't much like—*or need*—company. He was perfectly happy to strike out alone; to spend hours and hours alone.

What Lou did with this time remained something of a mystery to Flucknor; although he often caught sight of members of the house staff meandering through the hallways, en route or returning from the Throne Room where they would deliver—or collect—a stack of tomes.

Sometimes there were so many books that they enlisted the aid of one of the innately carved rosewood trollies from the Library itself.

Flucknor allowed himself a long, gaping breath before he reached up and knocked on the Throne Room doors. He waited for the response and then went in.

As it had been since recent memory—at least *Flucknor's* recent memory—the glass dome in the roof of the Throne Room was left uncovered and daylight beamed down on the stone slabs of the chamber; and onto the throne itself.

Lou was already sitting on the throne, his eyes fixed on Flucknor.

Unshifting.

Flucknor wondered if—*somehow*—Lou had found out about his kidnap and was going to demand an explanation from Flucknor, as if it had somehow been his fault.

But, instead, Lou pressed his lips together tightly, squeezing all the blood from his mouth, before saying, "You're to go out on a visit this afternoon."

Flucknor took a few steps closer, feeling the sound of the soles of his shoes dampened against the crimson velvet rug draped over the floor which approached the throne.

"Very well," Flucknor replied, unsure what else to say.

It wasn't like he was *permitted* any sort of opinion.

Flucknor waited for the longest time, feeling the silence open up between them. He wondered if Lou had something else to say; if he had been bottling up some other nugget of information to throw to Flucknor as if he were some sort of rodent searching the bones in a tavern back alley for the tiniest remaining scrap of meat.

Lou often liked to play this way . . . subtly showing off the depth and breadth of his knowledge to Flucknor, and—by so doing—prove his dominance over him once and for all.

"I should like you to report back," Lou added.

Flucknor furrowed his brow but said nothing in reply.

He couldn't quite grasp what Lou was getting at when he said 'report back' in the sort of tone which might be reserved for the inner workings of the Eye: the spy network which ran through the whole of Shellacnass like a chain of worker ants.

Everything got back to the King.

Lou turned his attention downward.

Only now did Flucknor realise that Lou had a book open across his lap. Although Flucknor tried his best to get a look at the cover, he was thwarted by Lou glancing back up and saying, "You can go now—the carriage is waiting."

20

A MYSTERIOUS DESTINATION

T HE WOODEN WHEELS of the carriage bobbed in and out of the ruts between the cobblestones. Flucknor was thrown about on the seat, despite gripping tightly to the handle above his head.

He peered out from under the glass, to the buildings which sprouted up out of the ground. All of them were uneven; like distended teeth in a rotten mouth. They grew toward the sky in seven or eight storeys.

Several times, Flucknor watched on as children rushed out from doorways and into the street without any apparent care for the oncoming carriage.

More than once, Flucknor felt his heart linger in his throat as he expected the carriage to mow down the children; to hear the morbid double *thud* as the fragile bodies passed beneath the wheels.

When the driver brought the carriage to a stop, Flucknor

peered at the building located beside them. He squinted at how it seemed to lean to the left or the right—he wasn't certain which, but it *certainly* wasn't pitched straight—then he poked his head out of the window and asked the driver to confirm that this was the correct location.

The driver simply nodded at the building then turned his head to spit out a wad of tobacco. "Borronder District," he said. "This's the place."

Flucknor hesitated a moment. He thought on the wisdom of arriving here—to Borronder District—in his High Representative's emerald-green robes with only an overcoat over the top.

When he leaped down and landed on the ground outside, he reached instinctively for the inside of his coat, for his dagger.

It was only after he'd been fumbling about for a minute or more that he recalled that his kidnappers had taken it off him . . . apparently when he'd been unconscious.

Flucknor couldn't suppress the smile which snuck onto his lips to think that he had managed to slash at one of his kidnapper's faces; and that he had caught them smartly across their skin . . . he wondered which of the Horrox he had cut open . . . he secretly hoped for Brotsboore.

As he made for the building, the driver asked him where he should wait and Flucknor replied with that old upper-class gem of 'just drive around'.

The building was made of wood and looked slightly unsteady in its structure.

Flucknor could tell where the scaffolds had been attached and where the builders had scrabbled about the exterior to get the support beams in all the right places. He was surprised that such constructions were to be found in Ilsnare. The Crystal City had not acquired its name by accident.

Flucknor often thought that the crowning achievement of Ilsnare wasn't the glass rooftops—as most people thought—but the sturdy, well-built, brick houses beneath.

And the years and years of craftsmanship which'd lovingly been dedicated to each and every construction.

Lou had instructed Flucknor to climb up to the seventh floor.

Just looking at it now, from the base, Flucknor couldn't help but feel as though he could witness the whole building swaying slightly from side to side.

But, he supposed, such was his status as Lou's right-hand man that he would need to clamber his way to the top. And *fie* to his own personal safety.

Flucknor was already out of breath by the time he'd reached the second storey, and couldn't quite comprehend having to clamber his way up another five of them.

But he pushed himself onward, telling himself that—like Rut and Sully—he was being sent off on his own little quest.

And that he *certainly couldn't* disappoint the King.

Once he had reached the top of the building, hearing the wooden planks of the stairs creaking beneath his every step, he felt the high winds blow back his hair; send it swirling over his shoulder.

There were several doors up here, and he had been told to enquire after 'Gdandra'.

With no other obvious course of action leaping out at him, he approached the first door and asked after 'Gdandra'.

He was informed that he should go two doors along, which he did.

When he knocked on Gdandra's door, he waited the longest time for a response, and, when none was forthcoming, he thought that he might've caught her on a day when she wasn't at home.

Already Flucknor could feel a slight sense of anti-climax lurking over him; having to go and 'report back' to Lou that he'd been unable to meet with her.

Flucknor, of course, would just have to return another day.

Feeling a slight fizz through his blood—something like a *kick* urging him on—he pushed up against the door and was surprised to find that it opened.

He glanced about him, looking to see if any nosey neighbours might be prying in the shadows, ready to demand that he leave their building.

But there was nobody there.

He stepped into the room.

21

A CONFRONTATION

S ULLY SAT hunched up on the log.

The campfire which the Glyph had started had now embered down into almost nothing.

He made a conscious effort not to meet Syre's eyes as she sat across from him; on her own log. But he had already taken note of how her dark hair, although never the tamest aspect of her, had grown ragged and wild; apparently from the journey through the Winter's Moan. Her cheeks, too, seemed to have hollowed out slightly and Sully supposed this to be the effect of—*like him*—not having eaten a hearty meal in a long while.

"So," Syre said, "would you mind running that past me again?"

Sully thought long and hard about how he might respond, but he was fairly certain that he had explained what had happened to him over the past few weeks in the very simplest terms that he could manage.

He drew a deep breath into his lungs and then sighed it out.

"I mean," Syre went on, "you're serious about *you* having made it this far into the Winter's Moan without any help—completely alone?"

Sully had decided to leave out the details about the Glyph, and Syre hadn't seemed to notice which suggested that she hadn't run into it when she had approached the cave. To be quite honest, the principal reason why Sully left out details concerning the Glyph had more to do with not wanting to come across as a *crazy* person . . . it could well be that he had merely imagined the Glyph. That he had had some sort of an 'episode'.

Being out in the wilderness could sometimes get like that.

Sometimes the solitude could get to him.

Often, out on the plains, Sully might ride for miles and miles and miles across deserted, undeveloped—*unworked*—plains of long grasses, only to feel that somebody was following.

Whenever Sully would glance over his shoulder, determined to catch the person who rode in his shadow, he would find himself disappointed—staring only after the plains which swept their way to the horizon.

The road he had already trodden.

He would never see anybody riding alongside him, of course, but the trauma which he had experienced since he had entered the Winter's Moan would surely be an understandable cause for him seeing someone—*something*—right now:

The Glyph.

Syre shook her head as she stared into the dying glow of the fire.

Sully thought of offering to reignite the blaze except for the fact that he had no idea where he might find some dry twigs—dry *anything* . . . the Glyph had taken care of all that.

Instead, he decided to turn the conversation around; to point it at Syre.

"What about you?" Sully said. "What're *you* doing way out here?"

Syre shrugged her shoulders. "I was looking for Lumbswich, but"—she jerked her thumb, apparently to indicate the stone which Sully and the Glyph had used to mark his grave—"I guess I got here a little too late."

Without thinking it through, Sully couldn't help blurting out, "Did Lou send you?"

Syre frowned. "Huh? No, no he didn't." Then she glanced up at him. "Did he send *you*?"

Here Sully felt his mind strain.

Throughout the telling of his journey thus far, he had managed to keep the motive from discovery. Now, however, it seemed that he was going to have to reveal everything.

He had really done it to himself . . .

"Yes," Sully replied, finally, "he told me that I needed to come here, to search for Lumbswich too."

"Why?" Syre shot back.

Sully thought about this for a moment.

Supposedly, Sully's mission was meant to be a secret; and he was to tell no one.

Syre, however, was Lou's sister . . .

"Lou wanted me to bring Lumbswich back to Ilsnare."

Syre wrinkled her forehead and then glanced beyond the fire, to the cave mouth. She gave a shake of her head, and Sully thought that she was going to further question Lou's motives.

Instead, though, she pointed to the opening and said, "What the hell is *that*?"

When Sully followed her finger, he saw that she was indicating the Glyph which—*a touch shyly*—was lurking at the cave opening; its lime-green glow holding back the night and making it almost impossible to miss.

22

VISITOR

AS FLUCKNOR passed over the threshold of the apartment, high up on the seventh storey, he felt a skitter move through his blood.

He knew what he was doing was wrong—that he was invading another person's home. And yet, dressed in his robes of the High Representative, he couldn't help thinking that what he did was justified . . . that he had the *authority* to be here.

The *King* had told him to come here, after all.

Flucknor glanced about the room.

Bookshelves; stuffed to bursting.

A simple table-and-chair set; made of cheap wood.

There was a desk arranged by the apartment window, and Flucknor could tell that thought had been put into its placement; in placing it where sunlight would beam onto the desktop.

On a set of shelves alongside the desk, Flucknor saw that there were many jars filled with varied and colourful liquids which he could just about make out in the gloom.

For some reason, he felt no desire to approach the jars.

The air smelled sharp and reminded him of the polish which the house staff would apply to the ornamental weapons which hung off the walls of the Palace corridors.

It sent a chill up his spine.

And it locked up his muscles.

But he trod further into the room, determined to complete the task which Lou had set him.

"Hello?" Flucknor said, hearing his call coming back at him.

The rooms apparently empty.

Only when he walked through a doorway, and into what turned out to be a bedroom, did he realise that the rooms weren't empty at all.

That, on the bed before him, there was a woman lying asleep on top of the sheets.

Blue-white hair sprouted from her scalp, reminding him of cotton.

The air was thick with lavender perfume and was so stifling that it brought tears to Flucknor's eyes just to breathe it in.

The woman's eyelids twitched in her sleep as if she had noted Flucknor's presence without even seeing him . . . as if she had *felt* him.

Before she opened her eyes, he knew that—like him—she had magic in her blood.

When she did look at him, he saw that her eyes were such a shade of grey-blue that they were almost transparent. She blinked several times—*long and slow*—apparently putting a great deal of effort into comprehending him.

Flucknor wondered what there might be about himself to comprehend.

He would've been the first to attest that he knew next to nothing about magic, and that his knowledge of worldly—*Mortal*—affairs were strictly limited.

How he had fallen on his feet—or fallen into *danger*—at the side of such a great mage as Louson Dorf often escaped him.

The woman raised a slight smile and then reached her hands out.

Flucknor took this as his cue to help her to her feet, and he did so.

He was surprised at how small she was when she stood before him.

"You must be Flucknor Arch," she said.

"Yes," he replied, feeling odd that she knew his name.

At first he presumed she had divined his name through some kind of magical means but, in the end, he decided that it was more likely that she had simply been passed the information by whoever had wanted them to meet.

Perhaps she had been given Flucknor's name by Lou.

"Gdandra?" Flucknor said, feeling that it would be polite to let her know that he knew her name also.

She gave him a slight nod—a smile—then she held out her hand and indicated the kitchen. "Tea?"

23

LIGHT

AS GDANDRA set about brewing the tea, Flucknor felt strangely calm, far calmer than he had felt on the way here when he hadn't known what might await him.

Now that it had turned out to be a sweet old lady, he felt that his anxiety had been put to rest for the time being. She had made him comfortable, told him to take a seat in her kitchen, in this easy chair with soft cushions and a nice view out of the window. He could just about make out the towers of Ilsnare Palace from here; where he had come from.

He could see the North-East Tower, where he had given Damon hospitality before Lou had unceremoniously kicked him out of the Palace. A little way further along, he could make out the long-ago abandoned North-West Spire. Then he could just about make out the dome of the Throne Room . . . where he had been that morning.

He switched back to his more immediate surroundings.

When he breathed in, he could smell the gentle scent of horse manure from the street outside mingled up with the warm, wafting odours of meat left to stew.

He supposed that all the housewives were in the throes of preparing their husbands' dinners for when they returned from work; whenever that might be.

From where Gdandra stood at the stove, fishing about with the iron kettle over the fire, her back to him, she said, "Do you usually enter strangers' homes without knocking?"

Flucknor felt himself paralysed for several moments.

Then he broke out of his daze.

"I, uh, did," he just about got out before noting the smile ripping apart her lips. "*Knock*, I mean," he added.

"Yes," Gdandra replied, "I know—I sensed that there was somebody at my door; that somebody had crossed the threshold." She gave a weak sigh. "But, unfortunately, there's only so much an old woman like me can do to defend herself in such a situation."

"Sleep?" Flucknor replied, again feeling a little dumbstruck by this conversation, and only noting the biting tone to his response a few seconds after he had uttered it.

Gdandra continued to work away at the kettle hanging over the exposed flames. Then, apparently finished with whatever it was she was doing, she turned back to him.

She narrowed her gaze slightly, in a way which took Flucknor off guard.

Her light-blue eyes seemed to cling to his flesh and to send a chilly sensation through his blood.

"You were sent to me for a purpose," she said, turning back to the kettle; the porcelain teapot ready and waiting—tealeaves seemingly already arranged within.

She took hold of the kettle's wooden handle and—with a slight grimace of either pain or exertion crossing her features—she poured a steady stream of boiling water into the pot.

Flucknor breathed in the thick, sweet steam of the tea, already feeling his mind being cast back to Ravensbark, and to all those times with the monks. He recalled how he and other apprentice monks would often come in from the snow outside after tending to something or other—usually the horses, in Flucknor's case— and that, in the Banquet Hall, they would find, more often than not, a whole succession of hot cups of tea arranged on the long wooden benches.

Just breathing in the tea which Gdandra was brewing here brought back all of those pleasant memories . . . of the fruit-and-berry teas . . . all of those delectable tastes he had long associated with the Sable Mountains and which, after year upon year of living in Ilsnare—*year upon year of city life*—he had almost clean forgotten about.

When Gdandra had finished with pouring the tea, she handed one of the cups to Flucknor and then eyed him momentarily. "Do you have any idea what that purpose might've been?"

Flucknor thought about it for a moment.

Turning his mind back to the question she had asked.

About the 'purpose' he might've been sent here for.

About what Lou had told him of this meeting.

That Flucknor was supposed to 'report back' . . . but about *what* he had no idea.

He decided it was better not to try and bluff Gdandra.

He shook his head.

"Ah," Gdandra said, a smile creeping onto her lips. "*Honest*, I like that." Her smile widened. She gazed down into her cup of tea.

"Modesty—even *false* modesty—is a rare attribute in a High Representative." She sipped at her tea and then eyed Flucknor over the rim. "I can tell the King has chosen wisely."

Flucknor hadn't much of an idea what to say to this, since, despite his meetings with the Council of Wisemen over the past few weeks, he really hadn't come to any different conclusion other than the fact that he most certainly *wasn't* suited to the role.

He simply didn't *fit*.

. . . Not that Flucknor's opinion mattered at all.

"Well, then," Gdandra said, after taking some more of her tea, "I suppose that you have learned something of your alignment along the Magical Field? About your place among the Four Corners?"

"Ice," Flucknor replied. "I have *ice* magic in my veins."

Gdandra again met his eyes then set her cup down. "Mm," she replied, still staring at him.

Flucknor caught the impression that he'd given the wrong answer.

Apparently sensing that Flucknor wasn't willing to make himself appear even more of a fool, Gdandra picked up the slack in the conversation.

"As I'm sure you know," she said, "there's more to magic than just fire and ice . . ."

When Flucknor sensed she'd drifted off, he suddenly realised that she wanted him to fill in the gaps, as if she was some sort of a school teacher. "Light and dark," he put in.

"Exactly," she replied.

He couldn't help but feel that her tone was somewhat sarcastic . . . that she was praising him for spitting out something which any self-respecting school child—*magically inclined or not*—would have had no trouble regurgitating.

Gdandra held up her withered, leathery palm so he might see. She illustrated with her index finger. "Whereas we all begin as either fire or ice; at one end of the horizontal spectrum"—she swept her finger downward and then quickly upward—"we also drift between the two ends of the vertical."

"Into lightness or darkness," Flucknor replied.

Gdandra beamed at him like an overly proud parent. "Yes, that's it." She continued to demonstrate with her palm. "The Four Corners; light, dark, fire and ice . . . we, as Magical beings, flutter from one extreme to the other; always struggling for equilibrium and yet seldom encountering it. We always end up somewhere—somewhere along the spectrum."

Here he decided he should butt in . . . just to make sure she didn't think him a *total* dunce. "Unless we stray too far," he said. "Either into fire, or ice; into the dark, or the light. Then our magic can destroy us."

Again, Gdandra smiled. "I can see you've been well prepared—at least as to the basics."

Flucknor speculated at how this was a long way from the truth.

And he wondered—vaguely—if this might be another of Gdandra's probing comments.

A double-edged sword.

Flucknor only realised that he had been staring at Gdandra's outstretched palm for several minutes when he thought to bring his cup of tea back up to his lips, and found that it had gone cold.

He winced slightly at the sensation and then, rapidly, turned his attention back to her.

"I'm sorry," he said. "I was sent here in an official capacity—

King Louson, he wanted me to 'report back' on my findings. Could you help me at all with that? Has something gone on? Something which the King should know about?"

Gdandra squeezed her palm shut and then laid her fist down in her lap, as if it was a tool which she was putting away for the time being but which could be easily retrieved at the appropriate opportunity. "Tell me, High Representative," she said.

"*Flucknor*, please."

Gdandra gave him a tight smile. "Have you any *acquaintances* about town who have taken a disliking to you—ones who have decided that you no longer belong among them?"

Flucknor, without being able to stop it, thought about the Creatures; about Brotsboore—how they had wrestled him off the street and taken him off somewhere . . . to *The Soore Whip?*

. . . They had made it very plain that he was no longer wanted; but that had been a different matter.

It'd been a case of pride, to put the matter simply.

They hadn't wanted anybody from the 'establishment' stepping on their moral high ground.

Flucknor turned his attention back to Gdandra's question and decided—*right away*—that he wouldn't be able to lie . . . it would be impossible.

This woman—Gdandra—could clearly read his every thought.

"Some," Flucknor replied, finally answering her question. "Some acquaintances."

Gdandra nodded. "And have you had any old friends—any old *masters*—visiting the city recently?"

Although he had attempted to put the episode of Damon—his old father abbot—out of his mind, he couldn't help but think of him almost every single day; to think of the old man struggling against the elements, struggling to find something *to eat* . . . but there was nothing he could do about it; Lou had made it clear who was boss in *this* town.

"Yes," Flucknor replied.

"And have you thought about *why* these Magical beings—others with magic running in their veins—have decided to cast you away . . . to keep you at an arm's length?"

"No," Flucknor shot back.

In truth, he felt himself growing a little impatient with the direction of the conversation. He had things to do. His responsibilities as High Representative meant that he had several matters to attend to back at the Galleries of Justice; 'responsibilities', as he had often joked about with the Council of Wisemen, of which Lou seemed utterly naïve . . . sometimes Flucknor wondered if it was easier to rule as king than to take on the role of High Representative.

"It's because you're different, Flucknor," Gdandra said, the smile which'd lined her lips for the entirety of their meeting slipping away for the first time.

Flucknor rose up out of his chair.

He glanced out through the window, seeing that his carriage was awaiting him.

"Thank you for meeting with me, madam," he said, "but I have other things to attend to before sundown. If you'll excuse me."

As he took a step toward the door, he felt the toe of his boot kick something.

With a *tinkle* of breaking porcelain, he had the presence of mind to look down.

His emptied teacup shattered into dozens of pieces across the wooden floor.

He glanced back at Gdandra, already feeling the cracks forming in the stern façade he was attempting to project. "I . . . I'm *sorry*," he managed to get out, and then continued on his way, stumbling more than once as he headed to the door.

When he did reach the door, Gdandra spoke to him in a firm, unshaking voice—none of the lightness to her tone from earlier. "There's a reason why Louson Dorf never taught you about magic, *Flucknor*. It's because he was afraid—because he *knows* who you are . . . who you *truly* are . . ."

Flucknor felt a fresh surge of blood—*anger*—to his temples. "What?!" he said, barking the word. "What *am* I?!"

But Gdandra just stood her ground, unmoving, her head inclined. "I think we'll be seeing more of one another," she said, and then, turning back to the stove where her kettle hung, she uttered, "Take care, High Representative—take *great* care."

24

A QUEST ENDS; AN ADVENTURE BEGINS

S ULLY LISTENED to the rhythmic *crunch, crunch* of footsteps through snow.

His muscles felt stiff and sore, and his heart seemed to bounce up into his throat and stick there with every one of his footsteps.

He had thought his body would adapt to the harsh conditions of the Winter's Moan, that, after several weeks here, he would have grown accustomed.

But, if anything, he felt that his surroundings were overcoming him.

Overwhelming him.

Just like always, Sully found himself at the back of the group, relegated to dragging about thirty or forty paces back from the advanced party of Syre and the Glyph.

Often, throughout the course of their journey together so far, Sully had found himself reflecting on his and the Glyph's relationship as compared with the one proceeding between the Glyph and Syre.

Whereas with Sully and the Glyph, their conversations had been kept to a minimum, and been frequently punctuated by the Glyph's unexplained disappearances—albeit disappearances followed by a return bearing some sort of food—the Glyph and Syre hadn't stopped talking from the moment they had met.

From the moment when Sully had introduced them to one another.

He supposed it was because this *Magical* business went over his head, and that his ignorance of the subject had been assumed, if not confirmed, by his silence . . .

Hence, he'd been left out of all discussion.

What made it all the more difficult was how Sully could still taste the delicious, seasoned roast pork the Glyph had prepared hours ago, by way of breakfast. Even now, with the light dimming on the horizon, he continued to experience the effects of a Really Excellent Breakfast.

He was more dependent on the Glyph than he wanted to admit.

Even to himself.

Once Syre and the Glyph had got past the normal, slightly awkward, getting-to-know-you stage, they had performed the firm shift into practicalities; into where they would be headed next.

When Syre had declared that, since Lumbswich was dead there was little reason for her to linger in the Winter's Moan, the Glyph had offered her its services in leaving the frozen wasteland.

Although Syre had claimed, at first, that since she had had little trouble in finding her way in, that it shouldn't be much of a mission to get out again, she had softened at the suggestion that the Glyph might be able to prepare all their meals and be an extra set of eyes.

The implicit message Sully detected was that the Glyph could also keep an eye on the stupid Mortal who was tagging along on their heels.

And Sully couldn't help but notice that the standard of the Glyph's cooking had *greatly* increased ever since Syre had joined the party.

He couldn't help wondering if the Glyph might be further along the masculine end of the scale than he had previously considered. Not an 'it' after all.

Because, and this was only Sully's experience, Mortal women held sway over all kinds of *male* Creatures; an inexplicable level of control which transcended magic itself.

So, here they were, all three of them headed out of the Winter's Moan.

And Sully, the perpetual loner he'd somehow become, lagging about like an unneeded third wheel on a horse-drawn cart.

Sully estimated that they were about a day's travel out from Lumbswich's home.

With the sun setting on the horizon, Sully wanted, more than anything, to raise the idea of settling down for the night; for them to search out a cave somewhere so the Glyph might start a fire.

But a mist had set in over everything and made their surroundings almost impossible to decipher.

He could hardly make out the Glyph and Syre up ahead . . . only the Glyph's faint, lime-green glow.

Right as Sully made a conscious effort to inject some sort of energy into his pace, to catch up on the advanced figures in his group, he felt a bitter, biting—*sweeping*—wind pick up and blow all across the piled-up snow.

It blew so strongly that Sully had to plant his feet firmly in the ground and stand still; afraid that it might knock him clean over if he kept up his progress in Syre and the Glyph's footsteps.

When the gust finally left off, Sully noted the lime-green light of the Glyph glowing out of the gloom up ahead. That it was growing brighter all the time.

Great, this was *just* what he needed . . . another chance for the Glyph to show what a *hero* he was . . . another chance for the Glyph to show just *how* hilariously out of his depth he was on this quest.

Just *what* Lou had been thinking when he'd assigned him to this task, he really couldn't say.

The Glyph, padding along at an alarmingly quick pace now, appeared out of the gloom; its lime-green glow almost dazzling in the darkness which'd somehow come to envelop Sully. "Quick," the Glyph said, its eyes near enough bulging from their sockets. "You must come *quickly*!"

Sully had no time to question, although he supposed that the very fact that the Glyph had spoken aloud—through its mouth rather than directly into Sully's mind—meant that something Very Precarious Indeed was taking place.

The Glyph took off at the same speed it had arrived. Sully took after it, feeling a childish sort of fear that there might be some cursed wolf—or a cursed *bear*—snapping away at his heels.

He supposed that he'd managed to get approximately four or five paces before the mighty wind howled over him once again.

This time he did lose his balance and take a tumble.

Although Sully had believed himself impossibly cold before,

he found a new *freezing* sensation set in over the surface of his skin.

Every muscle in his body seemed to lock up and his teeth began to chatter together so hard that he could hear them reverberating about his skull.

He strained his eyesight, hoping to catch the lime-green glow of the Glyph, but all he could make out was the sallow moonlight shining down through the fine mist.

An impossibly harsh wind blew over his body.

Already, he could feel the snow piling up over him.

Weighing him down.

He knew that if he didn't find his feet soon—if he didn't hoik himself back upright—that the weight would become too much.

It would *crush* him.

And yet Sully couldn't *quite* find the strength.

He couldn't *quite* lift himself.

As he lay on his front, face down in the snow, he wondered if this might be the way he was supposed to die; that the gods, in their infinite wisdom, up in the heavens, had decided that he would succumb to the freezing-cold conditions of the Winter's Moan on some forsaken quest of Lou's devising.

More and more snow piled upon him. He remained where he was.

It was while he lay there, thinking the blood in his veins would soon freeze, that he heard—clean and clear—a *roar*.

When he looked back on the event, he wondered if it was the *roar* or the hard shockwaves passing through the ground which finally convinced him to get up.

To set himself back on his feet.

Perhaps it was a bit of both.

What *was* for certain was that he still clung to life sufficiently that he found the strength to push himself back upright; to bound off in the direction that the Glyph had disappeared.

Maybe Sully would've kept on running all night, feeling those vibrations passing through the ground, and that mighty *roar* coupled with the pounding gales of wind at his back, if it hadn't been for the sure, solid hand which'd reached out from the mist and seized hold of the front of his tunic.

Dragged him in.

Before Sully quite knew what was happening, he found himself in a cave—much as he might've imagined it; albeit sans fire—and with the elements outside.

Looking around himself, the location illuminated by the lime-green glow of the Glyph, Sully couldn't help but notice that there didn't seem to be a way into the enclosed space.

His confusion was answered by the knowing look he received from Syre.

He realised she grasped the front of his tunic tightly in her fist.

She held a finger up to her lips, while Sully turned his attention to the Glyph; at his feet, its ear pressed up against the cave wall.

Finally, the Glyph pulled itself away.

It looked to Sully and Syre, and then said, "We have stirred a great evil—one which has dwelled here, in the Winter's Moan, for many centuries."

Before Sully could say anything and before the Glyph could confirm this 'evil's' name, Syre muttered, under her breath, "*Day'gatarn.*"

25

LEARNING IN THE LIGHT

ALTHOUGH the day after Flucknor had first met with Gdandra he had been instructed to 'report back', he had been unable to locate Lou anywhere in Ilsnare Palace.

Even the house staff were unable to tell him where the King might be; or even if they'd seen him leave the Palace.

He had gone through times like these—over and over. He knew that one thing was for certain: if Lou didn't want to be found then there were certain things that he might do in order to disappear.

And Flucknor would waste no time in looking for someone who didn't want to be found and who had the capacity—if they so willed it—to disappear *forever.*

Flucknor had much to do in the Galleries of Justice; many responsibilities which he, as High Representative, needed to attend to . . . if the King of Shellacnass wanted to play hide-and-seek games all the while then that was his prerogative.

One day, as he was working to clear out his office—he had allowed his desk to become an awful mess with parchment coming and going all over the place—he heard a knock at the door.

He immediately straightened up, feeling the tingle of dust which had caught at the back of his throat during his tidying. The dust bothered him so much that his voice must've sounded hoarse as he answered the knock; as he asked the person to come in.

There, standing in the doorway, had been a small girl; dressed in clothes which were spun of poor material, and yet—*surely*—the finest thing she had to wear.

In her hand, he saw, she clutched a scroll.

A message.

Although he was certain that she didn't quite understand the *complete* importance of his role—just what he meant for the city of Ilsnare—he could tell, from her pallid complexion, and how she shook slightly when she handed him the scroll, that she was terrified of him . . . of the task which'd been given to her.

Flucknor took care, as he always did with small children, to smile widely, and to generally make himself as *friendly* as he might manage.

Whether or not he succeeded, he couldn't have said.

But the small girl at least raised a slight smile to him as he slipped the scroll out from her tight fist. She promptly dashed off down the corridor, her job done.

Neglecting the small matter of leaving herself available to carry a response to the sender of the scroll. Or of acquiring a few grung from Flucknor for her troubles.

She would learn, though.

Flucknor brought the scroll over to his slightly tidier desktop, and he laid it down over the scratched-up walnut surface. He squinted as he stared down over the scrawling letters all written out there, half expecting this to be a fresh correspondence from Syre.

But it wasn't from Syre.

It was from Gdandra.

That old woman who he had visited a while ago, on Lou's request.

To think of her, to think of her house, brought back the fact that Lou was nowhere to be found; that he had made himself scarce the day Flucknor had gone to see Gdandra.

Flucknor skimmed the message, noted that she wished to meet with him this very evening.

He gazed out through his window, to the glass rooftops already catching fire with the setting sun, and hearing the dreary toll of the bells announcing the end of the working day.

He had a prior arrangement this evening; and one which he would very much like *not* to break.

In fact, it involved the Council of Wisemen.

Although the King was often indisposed—for obvious reasons —when light-hearted social occasions were floated, it was here that the High Representative was supposed to attend in the King's place; as a sort of ear for the King. A set of *eyes*.

The Council of Wisemen hoped to hold a feast, in honour of the Turning Season, and Flucknor had, long ago, accepted the invitation.

For him to neglect such an invitation—and at *such* short notice —would be tantamount to a Royal Snub . . . and *this* when Flucknor felt that his rapport with the Council of Wisemen was at an all-time high.

The whole point of Lou appointing Flucknor as High Representative had been so that Flucknor would stand confidently in his
place. It was, in short, an acknowledgement by Lou himself that he
simply wasn't cut out for these kinds of pompous events, or any
sort of social interaction that required any degree of tact.

To think of how Lou had treated Flucknor—how he had
prohibited him from so much as leaving the City Walls—just went
to show how Lou could act the role of the Petulant King to
perfection.

And that was the least of the treatment Lou had administered
on the Council of Wisemen whenever they had done something
against his taste.

In a way, Flucknor thought to himself, as he looked back down
at the scrap of parchment which Gdandra had sent him, him
going out of his way to ignore this batty old woman might well be
his own personal rebellion against Lou.

It would go to show Lou that, wherever he was hiding out—
and, no doubt, watching from—he couldn't control him with fear
forever . . . he couldn't play him like some child.

Although Lou had no sons, and their ages were, in reality, too
close together to ever have had that sort of relationship, Flucknor
often believed that Lou saw him as the child he'd never had.
Perhaps the father-son relationship had come about because Lou
had become battle-hardened early in life.

It was true that Lou's hair was already sprouting greys whereas
Flucknor's was still thick and lusty.

Flucknor wondered if Lou held a sort of envy for him; and the
life which apparently lay ahead.

Well, if Lou *really did* envy Flucknor his life then he was surely
doing a good job of blocking him from living it.

Flucknor stared down at the parchment before him, on his desktop, and he toyed with the idea of crunching it into a ball and tossing it into his office fireplace—just as he had done with the message from Syre.

But, instead, he slipped his overcoat off its hook, deciding to leave the parchment where it was.

If Lou truly was lurking in the shadows somewhere—*somehow* —then let him see the parchment spread out there on the desktop . . . let him see that it was just another scrap of paper . . . let him *see* that Flucknor wouldn't obey him.

Not any longer.

26

DINNER BECKONS

S AT IN THE HORSE-DRAWN CARRIAGE, on his way to the
Great Hall where he would be meeting the Council of Wisemen, Flucknor couldn't quite manage to keep himself still.

His leg—*quite apart from himself*—jiggled up and down as if
channelling some unspent energy.

He attempted to distract himself by peering out through the
carriage window, at the passing cobblestone streets; at the many
passing houses.

As he felt the vibrations of the carriage move beneath him, the
familiar, constant *wobble* of the carriage's springs over the cobblestones, he breathed in the thick scent of leather which clung to the
inside.

He thought that he could smell a slight odour of fish, too,
although he wondered if that might just be the ageing of the
leather, or some sort of substance which the driver used to clean

the upholstery. Something about the smell sent a quiver through his gut.

It set an almost *uncontrollable* sensation in him.

At first, he couldn't help but turn his mind to what he'd eaten that day; wondering if he might've consumed something which'd ended up making him feel rotten. But, once he'd finished his mental inventory of everything that'd passed his lips in the previous twenty-four hours, he was struck only by there being nothing remarkable.

In fact, he had hardly eaten anything; in anticipation of the feast which awaited him.

Before, when he'd been up in his office awaiting the end of the day, he'd been feeling excited about the food to come . . . *great anticipation* . . .

Since the girl had brought the scroll, though, he had begun to feel nauseous.

Several times, he'd been on the point of shouting out for the driver to bring the carriage to a halt, so that he might bolt out through the door and empty whatever his stomach contained.

But he held it in.

He knew that it wasn't natural for him to disobey Lou, and yet, at the same time, he knew that he *needed* to do this. He needed to show Lou that he wouldn't be pushed around any longer . . .

Lou might've made Flucknor High Representative believing that he would simply be his mouthpiece—his eyes to see with and his ears to hear with—but Flucknor was determined to be his own man.

And that went for his magic too, because Flucknor could feel, for the first time in years and years, that the ice was beginning to prickle in his veins once again.

Urging him to do something about it . . .

Urging him to *let out* what he kept locked away within.

Once again, Flucknor's wonderings turned to thoughts of jealousy on Lou's part; that Lou had wished to keep Flucknor weak, to prevent him from rising to challenge him one day.

Flucknor knew that Lou lived—if not in *fear* then at least in *anticipation*—of a magical war brimming on the horizon.

It could happen anywhere.

At any moment.

That was why Lou kept the Webbing Armoury close, albeit hidden . . . so that, at a moment's notice, he might be able to claim the Webbing Blade, Bow and Cloak, and take on anybody who might be *foolish* enough to challenge him.

As Flucknor turned this all over in his mind, still in the carriage, he felt the nausea desert him and a new, dawning understanding begin to surface.

He was afraid—he had *always been* afraid . . . afraid of Louson Dorf.

King Louson of Shellacnass.

The carriage turned the street corner.

Flucknor thought about how he might be able to shift this fear; how he might be able to crunch it down into a ball and toss it into a fireplace.

But those thoughts were interrupted when, up ahead, Flucknor saw the Great Hall—the fine centrepiece of the Crystal City —surrounded in ever-rising flames.

27

DAY'GATARN

S ULLY LEANED IN closer to the warmth of the fire—the fire which, despite the Glyph and Syre's Magical abilities, Sully had been called upon to spark into life.

It seemed, from what Sully knew of Syre and the Glyph, that they weren't up to much wherever fire was concerned; the other side of that being that they didn't seem to mind the cold as much as Sully did.

Sully had used the flint-stone kit and kindling which Syre had brought along on her travels, tucked away in her rucksack. Soon enough he managed to get a fire going.

He had surprised even himself with his fire-lighting ability and —truth be told—he had expected to receive a few more kudos than he had currently been granted.

Indeed, all of Syre and the Glyph's attention was focussed on the stone walls of the cave; varyingly pushing their ears up against the surface, listening out for the monster.

For this 'Day'gatarn' as Syre had phrased it.

Even though the cave was walled in on all sides, Sully could hear the wind howling outside.

And he thought he could hear the muted *roar* of the Day'-gatarn too.

Every couple of minutes, he convinced himself that he felt the same vibrations passing through the ground; shaking him all the way up the backs of his calves, and then, by way of his body's response, sending a shiver dancing down his spine.

Finally, as the firelight flickered about the inside of the cave, Sully watched on as Syre peeled herself away from the wall. She straightened up, then looked to the Glyph—still emitting its odd lime-green glow—before allowing her legs to go limp and for the rest of her body to slump to the floor. Apparently out of exhaustion.

He padded across the floor to help her up.

She seemed dazed to begin with, but she soon accepted the hand he held out to her.

And he helped her back onto her feet.

"Thanks," she replied, under her breath, shakily treading away from him.

As she retreated to the other side of the cave, Sully couldn't help noticing how a hardness seemed to form across her cheeks; how an anger appeared to brew behind her eyes.

He wondered who that anger was directed at; because who could hold *fire* in that sort of contempt?

Although Sully wasn't one to indulge himself in court gossip, he certainly wasn't above overhearing the murmurings of what went on, and he could recall, on many occasions, hearing about how Syre had been carrying out a romantic affair with Flucknor;

Lou's most trusted aide . . . beside Sully himself, and Rut, of course.

Was that the reason why Syre had left Ilsnare behind?

Wanting to break Syre's obviously tormented concentration on the flames, Sully found himself saying, "What're you doing all the way out here? I mean, how come you're not back at Ilsnare?"

Syre held her smouldering glare on the fire before turning her attention upward, to Sully. "You didn't hear about it—did you?"

"About what?" Sully said, frowning.

Syre went on to explain to Sully about how she had been responsible for saving Ilsnare Palace; how she had been the one to stop not only the assassin when he had escaped but the butler —*Tineoots*—who had transformed into his true self; a Creature . . . one which Syre described as being called Horrox: shapeshifters.

Sully could hardly believe it when she went on to tell him that Lou had decided to make her an outcast; that he had exiled her from Ilsnare.

The biggest question he wanted to ask was *why* . . . and yet he didn't want to pry into the matters between a sister and a brother; especially where magic was concerned . . .

While Sully sat by the fire, absorbing all that Syre had told him, he wondered what their next move would be; what they would do with the Creature—the *monster*.

Would they simply sit tight here and wait for it to go away?

Surely there was some other—*more proactive*—solution?

Just then, the Glyph removed its earlobe from the wall and looked over the campfire to Sully.

Before he even spoke, a smile snaked out across his lips.

"You know," it said, still speaking aloud rather than into Sully's mind, "what we could really do with now is some *bait*."

28

FIRE

A T FIRST, the driver of the carriage, apparently not having noticed the Great Hall or—more to the point—the gargantuan flames surging up over the entire building, continued to steer Flucknor forward, over the cobblestones.

In fact, before the driver had a chance to react—to slow the carriage—Flucknor was unhitching the door handle and slipping himself out and down onto the street outside.

The heat was almost unbearable. It singed the sides of Flucknor's face. His ice magic prickled beneath the surface of his skin.

Whenever he breathed in, he caught ash at the back of his throat.

It tickled his nostrils.

Lingered in his lungs.

Forced him to double over and cough.

Nearby—*too close*—he heard the *whinnying* of the horses which'd been driving his carriage, and the unmistakable sound of splintering wood . . . of the carriage wheels coming apart from the force of impact onto cobblestone.

The glass from the windows shattering into a thousand pieces.

Flucknor didn't need to turn around to know that the carriage lay on its side, that the driver, no doubt, had leaped clear to avoid being brought down with his transport.

When Flucknor straightened up, turned his attention to the Great Hall, he couldn't see anything except for the flames. The *wall* of fire which sprouted up out of the ground and seemed to blaze toward the sky as if being called by some god—or *collection* of gods—intent on reclaiming something of the Earth for their own.

People—some of them dressed in servants' robes, and others in more decorated clothing—rushed out of the building; not stopping to look back as they fled for their lives.

Smoke plumed from the windows, and Flucknor could hear the screams resounding within.

As he stood there, still stunned by the spectacle, he felt a single drop of sweat roll down between his shoulder blades; all the way to the waistband of the trousers he wore beneath his robes.

He thought about turning around and running away.

About fleeing for his own life back along the street.

The way he had come.

Who would know him when he wore an overcoat covering his emerald-green robes?

Nobody would *expect* the High Representative to put his life on the line.

To dare to rush into a burning building.

And perhaps that was what kicked him forward.

Because—right from the start—Flucknor had known he wasn't like the ordinary High Representative . . .

He weaved between those fleeing the building, doing his best to dodge out of their way, and clashing with several of them.

He tilted his head upward.

To the windows.

All he could see were flames.

He wondered if this was what *hell* was like.

Could it be any hotter?

As he got closer and closer to the building, his veins seemed to spring with an itchy sensation, but one which wouldn't be cured with something as cursory as a scratch from his fingernails.

No, it was a sensation far beyond his control.

One which controlled *him.*

He shoved in through the entrance of the Great Hall, against the bodies all bundling to escape the inferno.

The ash and smoke became almost too much to bear.

He brought his hands up to cover his nostrils and mouth, but that wasn't enough. He could still feel the strangling effect of the smoke.

He bowed his head, getting down beneath the level of the constant clouds.

He saw many stampeding legs, all of them headed his way.

For the exit.

Almost right away, Flucknor spotted a body lying prostrate —*unconscious*—on the staircase which led upward.

He rushed to the body, grabbed hold of it beneath the armpits.

When he felt the weight, he could tell that it was a man.

From the way he was dressed, in once-white clothing, he

supposed him to be one of the chefs . . . one of those who, all having gone well, would have prepared their meal.

He dragged the unconscious man, his heels scuffing across the tiled floor, all the way out.

Before he could look around—work out what he needed to do —he felt other hands helping him.

Taking the weight from him.

He heard voices.

Telling him to leave.

To go with them.

To *get out*!

But, without a second's delay, he turned back into the building.

Because something told him—something within his *blood*— that there were others who were still alive. Others who needed saving.

29

SURVIVORS

FLUCKNOR GRABBED HOLD of the banister and dragged himself up the staircase.

He felt twice as heavy as he had down on the ground.

His eyes ran with tears from the smoke and he felt as if the clouds of it weighed down his clothes. As if—whenever a fresh wave entered his body—it dragged his feet all the more.

But he kept on going.

Forced himself forward.

He knew that the prickling sensation in his veins wouldn't let him rest.

When he reached the top of the staircase, he glanced both ways, back along the landing, to the closed doors . . . and then he looked the other way.

Something—*something in his blood*—told him to rush off in the latter direction.

That this was where he would find the survivors.

He trusted the feeling.

The heat was almost unbearable here.

Already, he felt as if it hadn't only dried out his skin.

But his throat too.

It'd stripped him of any moisture.

Would it evaporate his blood if he didn't hurry?

Had it already begun to evaporate his blood?

He found himself confronting doors.

He shoulder barged them.

They were all locked.

Inside or outside?

He had no time to know the answer.

No time to beat his fists against the doors for a reply.

He had to rush onward.

When he reached the end of the corridor, he paused.

He stood stock-still.

The sensation swilling in his blood—*prickling his veins*—told him he was close.

That he needed to investigate this area.

That he *would* find survivors.

He turned around, looking for some clue.

Finally—*finally!*—it leaped out at him.

A door.

One of many; one of many *anonymous* doors.

All these secret meetings.

All these secret goings on.

Upmarket merchants.

Visiting nobility.

Quietly sitting councils.

All here . . . all of them hidden away.

He took several steps backward, and then he threw himself at the door.

It didn't shift.

He threw himself at it another time.

Again, nothing.

When Flucknor prepared for a third attempt, he took a moment to focus on the swilling—*chilling*—sensation within his blood.

He focussed in on himself, centring all the blood in on his heart.

Holding it there.

Holding it . . .

Finally, he broke from his mark; propelled himself *forward* . . . into the door; hearing the distant *crunch* of wood as it was ripped from its hinges.

Smoke billowed out in unstoppable clouds.

It swallowed everything.

He allowed it to rush over him, as if it was nothing but fresh, clean, summer air . . . *mountain air* . . . like it had been back at Ravensbark; those early-morning, frosty walks he would some-times take. Just him, and the horses, and the Sable Mountains stretching out on all sides . . . all those infinite possibilities; the entire world open to him . . . while he had been there, in the monastery, with only monks for company . . . a life . . . a life . . . *wasted* . . .

He caught his thoughts.

Snapped his mind to the task.

Smoke was everywhere.

Blackness absorbed *everything.*

Again, he sunk down low, beneath the level of the smoke.

He took several gulps of the clearer air.

But it wasn't enough.

Not enough to keep his thoughts sharp.

Not enough so that his brain kept ticking.

His blood, though, urged him onward.

Deeper into the blackness.

Into the smoke.

He sensed the scattered bodies, collected about his feet.

Many of them—*too many of them!*

Too many of them for him to carry . . . to drag from the Great Hall . . .

He settled on one body.

He didn't know how.

But he stooped low over it.

This one was light, easy for him to grasp hold of.

A woman?

Just as with the previous body, he hooked this one beneath its armpits, dragged it out onto the landing.

Already, he regretted his choice.

That he was unable to bring others with him.

But what could he do?

If he hesitated now they would all die . . . *no survivors* . . .

Thinking quickly, he dragged the body along the landing.

The smoke clawed at his eyes.

Whenever he breathed in, he found himself stuck in a half dream, praying that he might have some clear air. But it remained smoky; clogging his lungs.

Soon—*sooner than he thought*—he found himself at the top of the staircase.

And then stepping down.

Several times, he felt himself stumbling.

As if he would cartwheel over backward.

Land in a heap.

Neck broken.

But he pushed himself to keep going.

Keep going on.

Only when Flucknor felt the hands around him—*helping hands*—did he finally give in; did he finally allow himself to relax.

The blood in his veins stilled.

Its job done.

For now.

30

BAIT

S ULLY had to admit that he could hardly recall the process which'd led him to be standing here, out in the searing cold; wind whipping all about him.

Serving as *bait* . . .

Snow bit at his cheeks.

He could no longer feel his fingertips.

Or his toes.

The Glyph's roast pork was a distant memory.

Gone.

Nothing warm remained.

Only the freezing temperature.

Sully thought about how Syre had reached out and laid her hand on his shoulder, told him that he could trust her; trust her *and* the Glyph . . . that they would keep him safe from harm.

Already, Sully was seeing the folly of having believed the

sincere expressions which'd sketched both of their faces. That folly might just cost him his life.

The word that the Glyph had used was 'bait' . . . the Glyph had been honest with him; as far as honesty went . . . and Sully—like an *idiot*—had gone along with it.

Sully glanced around, into the chilly mists, seeing his breath form before his face.

He couldn't *see* the monster anywhere; couldn't see the Day'-gatarn at all.

Then again, from what Sully had learned of monsters throughout his life, he knew that the very best of them—or at least the *fiercest*—often believed remaining invisible, or as close to it as possible, an extremely high-value virtue.

The fact that Sully couldn't hear the previous *stomping* sound from before also served to raise his spirits; and neither could he hear the open-throated *roar* from earlier.

Might it be that the monster had simply . . .

Right then, Sully heard the advancing footsteps.

The *crunch, crunch, crunch . . . CRUNCH!*

Sully's heart beat against his throat.

His mouth tasted bitter.

All his muscles seized up.

He pivoted around—desperately *hoping* that he might be able to catch a glimpse of the monster.

But he could see only the mist.

He knew the monster was close.

That—*most likely*—it towered above him.

He thought he could sense heat.

On his skin.

Its *moist, warm* breath.

A faint stench of well-worked Mortal feet.

For several long seconds, he wasn't panicked at all.

He was calm; and comfortable.

But the sensation didn't last.

31

HERO

WHEN FLUCKNOR WOKE UP, he was confused.

The whole world was bleary; thick with a bright, white light.

It stung his eyeballs.

Seemed to fire right to the back of his brain.

The sensation tormented him for an age.

Or so it felt.

Only when he breathed in the thick, heady—*sharp*—stench of medicine did he realise that it had really happened. That it hadn't been a dream. That he *had* been in the Great Hall . . . and that the whole building had been on fire.

And that he was still alive.

He brought his forearm up to cover his eyes from the sun's glare.

When he finally managed to focus, he realised that whoever had put him to bed the night before hadn't thought to shut the curtains. He supposed that there'd been a panic; that certain things had been forgotten in the rush.

He turned to look at his bedside table.

He was *back* at the Palace.

Back in his quarters.

A variety of glass vials stood sentry on his bedside table; all multi-coloured liquids within:

Unnatural greens, blues and yellows.

When he padded his bed—*his surroundings*—he realised he was only in his underclothes, and, when he breathed profoundly, he couldn't quite tell whether or not his clothes still stank of smoke or if he had taken the smoke so deeply into his lungs that he would be smelling it forever more.

Until the day he died.

He turned his attention to the doorway.

He could hear footsteps.

His heart bounced about his ribcage.

When he felt the ice magic bristle about his blood, he could hardly stay still. He could hardly keep himself from shucking his sheets and standing.

But something about the person approaching—something about the echo of the footsteps out in the corridor—told him that he needed to stay put.

That he couldn't get up.

Not quite yet.

There was a distant, muffled knock on the door and Flucknor realised that his hearing, too, had been affected by last night . . .

Had the smoke done that to him, or was it the ice magic writhing through his veins, unwittingly damaging Mortal parts of his body with its strength?

He remained silent, knowing that, in his current condition, he wasn't expected to answer the enquiring knock. He waited, allowing his eyelids to droop, watching the door of his quarters.

Waiting to see who would pass through.

His heart gave another kick as he saw who it was.

It took his brain another second or so to really understand.

To *truly* understand.

It was Lou.

Louson Dorf, King of Shellacnass.

Flucknor held his eyelids shut.

He had believed, even back when he was at the Great Hall, when all those people were rushing free of the burning building, that Lou had been watching him.

Well, he *was* watching him now.

Lou paced into the room.

"What happened?" Flucknor said, his voice sounding weak and distant. "Last night."

Lou didn't turn right away. He continued to approach the bedroom window and look out, down onto the glass rooftops which Flucknor couldn't see from where he lay in bed. When Lou didn't reply, Flucknor decided to ask another question.

"How long have I been sleeping?"

This time Lou did reply. "About a day," he said. "The wise woman who came, she said that you've suffered from breathing in smoke." He turned away from the window, his attention now focussed on Flucknor, a slight smile tweaking his lips. "Don't worry, you'll live, I'm sure."

It was the smile, more than anything, that had Flucknor feeling warm inside.

It'd been a long time since he'd seen Lou smile.

An *awfully* long time.

Sometimes, Flucknor found himself wondering if Lou was really as miserable as the picture he painted of himself . . .

If Lou wished to project himself as some kind of dejected martyr then he was a blazing success.

Then again, Flucknor didn't quite know what it might feel like to have the whole world sitting across his shoulders; weighing him down.

And, since Lou never spoke to him about any matter of import, he supposed that he would never truly know.

"They're saying you're a hero," Lou said, turning his attention back to the rooftops.

Flucknor remained still.

What was he supposed to say to that comment?

It was anybody's guess what might be on Lou's mind now.

Could he be thinking of the many citizens of Ilsnare who all depended on him?

Who thought of Lou whenever they heard loud *bumps* in the night?

Who believed in Lou as a protector more capable than a thousand Royal Guards?

. . . Another thing which Flucknor would never know.

Never *truly* know.

That same smirk from before continued to cling to Lou's lips.

He gave a slight shake of the head.

"Hearing about it," Lou said, "brought back memories."

" 'Memories' ?" Flucknor replied, feeling as if just the word itself was distant and whimsical.

"Yes," Lou said, "about when my village burned down, when Endmere burned down."

"What happened?" Flucknor said.

Lou remained very still for a long time.

Then he reached out and clung to the brass railing at the window. "*Hildie,*" he said.

Even though Lou had spoken Hilda's name in its endearing form, Flucknor couldn't help but sense that sting of bile which clung to it.

Which would *always* cling to it.

Lou's gaze remained lost in the rooftops for a long time, and then he turned back into the room.

He glanced to Flucknor, gave another of his unconvincing smiles, and then stalked off toward the door. "You'll have another visitor in a few minutes if that's all right?"

But Lou left the room before he gave Flucknor a chance to reply.

Thinking about it later, Flucknor supposed it hadn't really been a question.

32

ANOTHER MORNING LIGHTNESS

FLUCKNOR LAY ON HIS SIDE, attempting to get his thoughts clear.

He stared vacantly out the window, to the overcast sky above.

He wondered if his new status as 'hero' might afford him the same liberty afforded the birds of Shellacnass.

Would Lou allow him on the other side of the City Walls?

He really wouldn't count on it.

Again, there was a knock at the door, and—*again*—Flucknor said nothing at all.

He eyed the figure who rounded the door and—for some reason; while he kept his eyes out of focus—he almost convinced himself that it was Syre.

That Syre had returned to Ilsnare.

That Lou had allowed her back.

No, it wouldn't be that easy . . .

Lou wouldn't allow Flucknor to leave the City Walls; and neither would he allow Syre to enter through them.

Their only hope of any sort of contact remained through letters, although even that had become an impossibility since Syre had headed north and out of range.

Away from Flucknor forever.

Only now did Flucknor take in the person who'd entered his room properly.

He saw her blue-white hair, with its consistency like cotton.

And he caught a whiff of lavender perfume.

Those grey-blue eyes ... even from across the room.

Gdandra.

Today she wore a set of golden robes; ones which Flucknor recognised as belonging to a certain group of Representatives at the Galleries of Justice.

The group of senior Representatives from which—among other important organisations—the Council of Wisemen were sourced.

And from who, Flucknor knew in his heart of hearts—*everybody knew in their heart of hearts*—the current High Representative should've been chosen.

Beneath her robes, he caught a flash of the crimson tunic, and he felt his heart pound a little harder. She hadn't told him who she was, or where she worked.

If he had known that she, herself, was a Representative—and so *important*—well, it might've made their previous meeting *different*...

How, exactly, Flucknor couldn't quite say for sure; although he was fairly certain that it wouldn't have ended with his storming out like some wronged mistress.

Gdandra seemed to recognise this as she approached his bed, a slight smile clinging to her lips. When she was close enough that they could speak in a near whisper—no more than half a dozen steps away—she said, "What you did last night was a wonderful thing."

Flucknor felt his cheeks burn.

He thought about preparing some sort of a self-effacing excuse, but couldn't bring one to mind.

In the end, he just stayed still, doing his best to keep a *pleasant* expression fixed across his face.

This old woman would be gone before long . . . and she would leave him in peace.

"What you felt," she said, and then reached up and placed her hand over her chest, "it was the lightness of your magic—that which dwells within you; that which has *developed* as your body has developed." She drew a breath, then exhaled, as if this was some sort of an impossibly heavy thing to even contemplate; let alone put into words. "All you had to do was follow the urge— follow your instinct. And that, let me tell you, is something which is difficult to achieve; something which only one in a thousand might achieve."

Again, Flucknor felt taken aback by all this golden light being cast on him.

He wished there might be some way to make her see that *instinct* was all it had been . . . that he hadn't *thought* about it really . . . hadn't had *control* over it really . . .

Gdandra batted a hand—apparently having heard him *think* this comment. "Please," she said, "control is the least of your worries when you have lightness like that running through your blood. Why should you want to control pure *goodness* in a world which is constantly buffeted by evil?"

He allowed this comment to pass, and then said, "Why did Lou want me to go and meet with you?" He waited a beat, and then it came to him, although it seemed so obvious; so obvious that, really, he didn't need to speak it. "He wants you to guide me—to show me the way?"

Gdandra nodded. "He is smarter than most—more *perceptive*. What the King realises, what he sees, is the limit of his powers . . . and how he might negatively influence the very differences which make up the richness of our world; and which create the very *strongest* of natural power."

Flucknor felt his mind swimming with the details Gdandra laid out for him.

And somehow he couldn't believe—he couldn't *believe* that there was such a simple explanation to how Lou had treated him throughout these years; how he had never indulged his questions about his magic . . . gone out of his way to avoid even the simplest of questions.

Now, though, Lou felt his mind snap back to another point.

To something far more tangible.

More grounded in the 'real' world, as he saw it.

"Last night," Flucknor said. "How many died?"

Here Gdandra's features darkened and the smile which'd dominated her lips for the entirety of their meeting finally dwindled.

"The one you saved was Leona; the Speaker of the Council of Wisemen." She shook her head. "The rest of the Council perished, I'm sorry to say." She brightened a touch as she added, "But you have to remember that you're still attempting to harness your power. Once you have dominion, your powers will outstrip even your wildest imagination. You can be the greatest force for *good* that the world has ever seen."

Flucknor felt the tightness settle over his chest once again.

And he had no idea how to shift it.

33

NESTING

WHEN IT HAD DAWNED on Sully that the Creature—
the Day'gatarn—had been standing over him, the world
had suddenly begun to spin . . . and then it had disappeared
completely.

The blackness had seeped in around the edges.

He had believed that he would never be able to see again.

That this Creature had—*somehow*—blotted out his vision
forevermore.

It'd been when Sully had awoken, and breathed in the rancid
stench of what he believed to be sweaty Mortal feet, that he knew
the Creature, at least, hadn't seen fit to kill him.

Not yet, anyway.

Or perhaps this was hell.

His own *personal* hell.

He shook off the sensation, and tuned in to his surroundings.

It was dark, with only the tiniest amount of daylight pene-trating the lair, and he could only make out suggestions of objects.

Of *shapes* surrounding him.

Several moments passed before he got the creeping sensation that the objects he could just about make out in the gloom were smooth, and slightly oblong. They reminded him of when he had been a child, living out in the countryside, and his father had ordered him to go about collecting the eggs from the chickens first thing every morning.

Sully still felt a strong sense of distaste for *that* particular task.

First for his father demanding that Sully get up so early, before the sun had risen. And while his father would remain in bed, still in a drunken stupor from the previous night.

Second, Sully would take stock of the grim nature of the job which awaited him.

How he would slip his hands in beneath the still-snoozing hens, feel the smooth shapes of the eggs. Several times the eggs would be smothered in excrement, or else broken under their overweight—*overzealous*—mothers.

And those were just the normal times when foxes hadn't got into the coop at night.

Sully's father always blamed him for any fox attack. Sully had always known for a fact that his father was *always* the last to check on the chickens at night; and that his clumsy drunkenness would be the cause of whatever catastrophe arrived in the morning.

It seemed that with each passing moment Sully spent in his father's company, he better understood why his mother had taken the decision to flee the home.

The only thing which stuck with Sully—which left him

wondering—was why she had seen fit to leave Sully himself behind . . .

Sully allowed his mind to drift back to the present.

He took in the area surrounding him again; this time with fresher eyes.

His vision had grown accustomed to the lack of light and he could now better make out the objects which surrounded him.

Certainly eggs . . . but much larger than a hen's.

To put it mildly.

As Sully eased himself off the ground, he felt a substance between his fingers, soft and doughy—slightly *warm*—and which reminded him of clay.

When he brought his fingertips up to his nose, gave the substance a sniff, he realised that it *most certainly wasn't* clay.

And that apparently the Day'gatarn shared at least one thing with hens when it came to nesting habits.

Sully kept himself distant from the eggs. He realised now that the eggs were only a little smaller than his full height; when he stood straight-backed with his chin neatly tucked into his chest.

He reached out and felt for the perimeter of the nest.

He found the smooth edge to it.

And he gripped onto the soft surface tightly.

Now that he thought more about the nest—about what it *consisted* of—he felt an uneasy, tight sensation grip hold of his stomach. Despite having grown up on a farm, he had always liked to keep his hands as clean as possible.

And, right now, his hands were certainly *not* clean.

As Sully hoiked himself upward, to the lip of the nest, he realised that he could hear the sound of movement in the distance; nothing more than the *rustle* and *trudge* of footsteps.

Although this didn't sound like the Day'gatarn, he wasn't going to take any chances.

This was his opportunity to get away from the Day'gatarn . . . and he would take it.

Once Sully had got himself out of the nest, and back onto the comparably firm, tightly packed dirt ground, he thought back to those promises which Syre and the Glyph had made him as they had forced him—that was the right way to put it, wasn't it?—into serving as their 'bait'; as their *means* to attract the Creature.

They had said that they would leap in right away, that once the Creature thought that it had Sully in its talons—*did the Day'gatarn have talons?*—then they would be able to focus their magic—their hexes, enchantments, or whatever else—and free him from the grips of the sinister monster.

Even though Sully had fainted before he could take in the *full* experience of his snatching, he felt that he caught the gist of what'd happened.

That the Glyph and Syre had failed.

And now all that remained was for Sully to die.

All of a sudden, bright light filled the nest.

Sully brought his forearm up to shield his eyes.

It was a brilliant, neon-blue glow.

One which seemed so unnatural—so *complete*—that it rendered Sully stunned.

And it was then that the situation became impossibly worse.

Because one of *them* spoke into Sully's mind.

— *Do not fear, Mortal; you shall be safe with us.*

Funnily enough, that message, as it arrived in Sully's skull, without intervention or cooperation from his ears, went precisely no way at all to reassuring him.

34

NIGHT-TIME AWAKENING

FLUCKNOR AWOKE to feel that the surface of his skin— even the skin beneath the undershirt which he wore to bed —was soaked in sweat.

It seemed to take a moment for the sensation of the chill to catch up with him—for the draught which rolled in around the door to come into contact with his drenched bedsheets.

"Flucknor?"

The voice was whispered; *husky* . . . and he felt a creeping sensation pass up his spine.

He turned his attention to the form at the door.

He knew who it was, of course. There was only one person who would dare to disturb the High Representative's sleep for any other matter than raising the alarm due to a fire:

The King of Shellacnass.

Louson Dorf.

Still struck with the dreams he'd been having, the flames which'd risen up to his throat and nearly melted the skin clean off his bones, Flucknor shucked his bedsheets and stumbled across the floor in the direction of Lou's voice.

"What time is it?" Flucknor said.

"*Late*," Lou shot back, and then paused, apparently in consideration. "Or *early*, depending on how you look at it."

Flucknor heard a slight smile in Lou's voice.

"What's going on?" Flucknor got out, halfway to his wardrobe.

Although Lou's night-time visit was a surprise, it wasn't exactly the first time that it had occurred. Indeed, even now, in his doped-up, sleepy state, Flucknor had the mental prowess to recall half a dozen occasions when Lou had arrived to his quarters in the dead of night, all dressed for action, and ready to go.

By now, Flucknor knew the drill.

Flucknor dug out a robe and then—pausing for a moment before selecting some surreptitious quilted armour to wear beneath—he shot Lou a sidelong glance.

He saw that Lou was dressed in light armour.

That he had on a light-weight breastplate; dulled with ash.

And that he wore a sword at his waist.

A crossbow dangling down between his shoulder blades.

"Come on," Lou said, his tone quickening, apparently losing his patience. "There isn't much *time*."

Still no more aware than he had been previously, Flucknor quickly shoved the quilted armour down over his head before tugging his robe on over the top.

Within his wardrobe, Flucknor took hold of his sheathed dagger, and strapped it to his waist.

He hadn't anything more substantial—weaponry-wise—within his own quarters.

Although Flucknor didn't doubt that a thief or assassin was a justified fear for someone of his status, he had a somewhat strangely placed fear of having his own weapons used against him.

He hated the idea of the blade of his own dagger being held up against his throat, and to have to breathe his last knowing that he was being killed with his own instruments.

When Flucknor glanced up again, he realised that Lou had already shifted on out into the corridor. Flucknor looked about his quarters, with the clear concept that he had forgotten something —that sense which always struck him when he was startled awake.

But he ventured on after his king all the same.

As had been the common thread through the times before when Lou had woken Flucknor in the middle of the night, there was no explanation of where they were headed or what they wished to achieve.

Flucknor was simply expected to follow.

Although Flucknor knew that Lou surely, with his Magical capabilities, had not only the ability to make himself invisible to Mortal eyes, but to transform himself into *beasts*, he apparently seemed content to skirt the shadows of the streets like some common mugger.

Flucknor wondered if Lou was perhaps cracking up, if he had maybe spent too much time alone and had taken to leaving the Palace only at night; to prey on citizens shifting their way through the city streets . . . living out some dual life as a *thief* just because it added some excitement to his routine . . . something besides all those books he read.

Most likely, though, Flucknor supposed that Lou was retaining his Mortal appearance so that Flucknor wouldn't be left behind if Lou was to transform himself into a street dog; or a *rat* . . . just as with everything magic related, Lou had always resisted passing on even the most fundamental information to Flucknor.

Glad to see him struggle in the darkness.

Or in the overbearing light . . .

The air was chilly, but this wasn't unpleasant given the dreams that Flucknor had been having earlier; the ones which'd seen him back in the Great Hall, with the flames all around him, springing up on all sides.

The soot in his lungs.

Heat up against his skin.

Unbearable . . . just *unbearable* . . .

"Fluck?" Lou said, pressing his back up against the street wall, his head angled toward Flucknor and his voice kept to that same whisper.

Flucknor said nothing as he sidled up alongside.

Seeing that Lou wished for him to follow his gaze—to look just where *he* looked—Flucknor did as was required.

He saw nothing at all.

Just crooked streets.

Houses on either side.

Some with sturdy, wooden-beam frames; and others which were simply put together out of plaster and whose roofs seemed to be wilting and sinking.

Through the crooked streets, Flucknor eyed the building

which was the focus of Lou's gaze. It took Flucknor a couple of moments to realise it, but, when he did, his heart nearly popped up onto his tongue and then out of his mouth.

Standing before the two of them, Flucknor realised that it was *The Soore Whip.*

35

SKIRMISH

WHEN FLUCKNOR turned his attention back to Lou, he could see that a stony, neutral expression had set in over his face.

Pure, unadulterated concentration.

"You were here before, weren't you?" Lou said, his face still in profile. "I had you come here, when you were with the Eye—to survey the meetings."

Since there was nothing for Flucknor to deny, and, more to the point, no reason for him to deny it, he gave Lou a staunch nod by way of an answer.

Lou went on, "Would it surprise you to know that we're standing only paces away from those responsible for the fire at the Great Hall?"

Flucknor's chest tightened.

His heartbeat raced.

When he answered, he nearly forgot to keep his voice to a

whisper. "I . . . I thought it was an accident," Flucknor said.

Lou shook his head. "No, an *accident* involving all the members of the Council of Wisemen is *far* too convenient for my liking. So convenient, in fact, that I believe it to be close to an *impossibility.*"

Flucknor stared on, at the façade of *The Soore Whip.*

He took in the smooth, slickly painted black wooden beams of the exterior, and then the snow-white painted plaster.

He had come here so many times—so many times *after* he'd completed his assignment.

For the longest time, Flucknor had believed himself to be nearly one of the Creatures . . . and that when the day came that magic was tolerated throughout Ilsnare and the Kingdom of Shellacnass they would walk side by side as *equals.*

Only standing here now, with Lou alongside him, did the realisation dawn on him that this vision would almost certainly prove impossible to occur in any reality.

And, at least to Flucknor's mind, if the Creatures had really had a hand in burning down the Great Hall; and in so doing ending so many Mortal lives . . . the lives of so many *citizens* of Ilsnare, then didn't they deserve to die in turn?

Flucknor had never been able to get himself shot of the profound sickness he felt whenever an execution was carried out in the Palace courtyard . . . but neither had he ever looked away from one he was compelled to witness.

There was something about an execution—an almost *holy* quality to it—which stripped the breath from his lungs and forced all his attention front and centre onto this real-life tragedy playing out before his eyes.

'An eye for an eye' might well have been the policy all

throughout Shellacnass, but Flucknor could never quite get over the joylessness of the task.

Something which felt as unnatural as sleighing fellow beings couldn't be right.

Could it?

"Come on," Lou said, grabbing hold of Flucknor's sleeve. "We'll catch them if we're quick."

36

THE HORROX

T HE WARMTH was almost unbearable.

Sully had known nothing like it.

He walked among the figures with the long, lizard-like snouts; and the rash-red skin.

The black eyes.

All of them wore sable robes, the hoods sagging back between their skinny shoulder blades, their hands hidden by the wide sleeves, and their ankles concealed by the dangling cloth.

Sully knew who these Creatures were, of course; he had learned about them during his visits to the Crystal City; to Ilsnare.

The Horrox was their name and Sully knew them as shapeshifters.

As those who could take on any form.

Their number was unknown throughout the Kingdom, for the simple fact that they could take on any sort of Mortal shape—any *animal* shape—and remain undiscovered.

The glow which they generated—in a similar fashion to the Glyph—illuminated the passageway they walked along. Instead of it being a lime-green glow, like that of the Glyph, the light was the same neon-blue which Sully had found consuming him back in the Day'gatarn's nest.

As far as Sully could make out from his surroundings, he saw that it was soil; that this was a dug-out tunnel. He wondered how far it might stretch.

While these ponderings occupied his mind, he realised that he could feel the overpoweringly *pleasant* warmth wafting its way up toward him.

Was that pork he could smell on the air?

If the Horrox didn't intend to kill him then it would be kind of them to feed him.

An ordeal like the one he'd just been through seemed to merit a feast.

Sully felt giddy. He supposed he was entitled to feel so . . . an awful lot had happened in no more than a matter of hours.

He'd been in mortal peril.

His friends had deserted him.

And now he was in the company—held prisoner?—by these Creatures.

Not that there was anything he could do now.

When he thought to count them, he saw that there were five.

Two ahead.

Two behind.

Another walked at his side.

No escape . . . not unless he wanted to rush back along the passageway in the direction of the Day'gatarn's nest . . . or—alternatively—sprint forth into the unknown; in the direction they were headed now.

And what would happen if—*best-case scenario*—he did manage to find an exit; a way which would let him back outside.

What was to stop the Day'gatarn tracking him down again?

Or to stop himself freezing to death before he became reunited with Syre and the Glyph?

As they continued their march on down through the tunnel, getting closer and closer to the warmth, Sully wondered just what the Horrox were doing up here, in the Winter's Moan; and whether they might be in cahoots with the Day'gatarn which'd captured him; which'd brought him back to its nest. Because of his fainting episode, he hadn't yet had a chance to so much as look the Day'gatarn up and down . . . was it a bird, a mammal . . . something *else*?

The mystery would remain unsolved.

The Horrox had brought him to the end of the passageway.

A doorway was marked with a pair of torches.

One on each side of the opening.

The darkness seemed to lead downward into the Earth.

Sully's vision was impaired for several seconds in the brightness of the flames.

Another *warm* waft blew against him.

This time he was convinced that he could smell pork . . . but it might just as easily have been the memory of the meal which the Glyph had cooked for him and Syre.

Sully trudged along, still feeling very much that he was being escorted.

During their journey along this passageway, Sully had kept

careful watch of the Horrox's state of mind, reminding himself to take stock of those who held him prisoner.

To see if he might garner any clues as to what they might do to him.

But, thus far, they had shown him nothing at all.

As they headed down further along the slope of the tunnel, Sully found his eyes straining to pick out the light ahead. He realised that the Horrox's personal—*Magical*—light source was beginning to fade. He wondered if they were tiring, or if this was intentional.

Finally, Sully got his head around the fact that—although the Horrox's light was waning—there was a new, stronger light taking its place.

A bright, yellow light.

Again, it took Sully a few moments for his eyes to become fully accustomed to the change in his scenery—the change in the light —and when they finally did take in what stood before him, he realised that he was in a throne room.

It was an enormous chamber, at least as large as the Throne Room of Ilsnare Palace; if not *larger*.

There were no windows here, being as they were, a long way underground.

Sully's eyes ran across the throne room walls. He saw that there were several doorways leading off from the chamber. He wondered which one of those would lead out to the Winter's Moan . . . and not to the Day'gatarn's nest . . .

A series of stone slabs, one leaning against the other, propped up a velvet, royal-red cushion.

On top of the cushion sat another Horrox.

Like the other Horrox, this one—apparently the leader—wore

a sable cloak.

It was odd now for Sully to note the way that the Horrox all wore their cloaks with the hood down. Whenever he had caught sight of Horrox in the past, on the streets of some village or town in Shellacnass, it had always been while they had their hoods drawn up; to hide their features.

Not until Sully had become a skuller, and seen all those Creatures which went *bump* in the night, did he learn the truth about many of those cloaked figures . . . the ones who he had always assumed to be hobblesmen. And never so much as *entertained* the suspicion that they might be Creatures.

He felt as if an invisible hand reached out and pressed its palm flat against his ribcage. He had no choice but to come to a halt.

When he glanced about himself, he saw that his Horrox escorts had done the same.

All of them peered up at the Horrox seated on the throne.

"Greetings," the Horrox said, out loud, rising up off its cushion. "I am so glad you could join us, Sulliman."

A harsh chill crept in about the collar of Sully's tunic, and, perhaps for the first time in the Winter's Moan, it wasn't due to the weather; it was because of fright.

Sully pushed the fear away, and held the Horrox's gaze. "How'd you know my name? What's happening here?" he said. "What're you *doing* here—this far north?"

Sully felt tension twist in the air of the throne room.

He realised this was an inappropriate thing—*in either tone or content*—for him to have said.

He wondered if the Horrox would allow him to take it back.

Instead of hurling a hex at him, though, the Horrox stood up, towering over Sully. It merely wore a wry smile and gave a shake of its head.

"My, Sulliman, you do have a lot of questions on your mind. A man who knows that time is a precious commodity and who would rather not waste it."

Sully held his ground, feeling his whole body tingling.

It wasn't fear now . . . it was something *else* . . . some kind of confidence?

Whether or not it might be misplaced, he would likely find out later.

All that mattered at this point—as Sully had well learned when dealing with Mortal land owners throughout Shellacnass— was that he needed to *appear* as though he had the upper-hand.

The five Horrox guards who surrounded him were almost beside the point.

The Horrox standing before him, on the stone, took several steps toward Sully; and Sully watched on to see how the Horrox tucked its hands behind its back as if this matter was nothing more consequential than a Sunday afternoon stroll in the park.

"Tell me, Sulliman, what makes you think that Mortals should control these lands?" It cocked its head to one side. "What makes you *believe* that Mortals are in some way superior to us . . . *Creatures*, as you term it."

Sully could feel the bile as the Horrox muttered the word 'Creatures'.

Just the sound of it seemed to pinch his skin into pimples.

"I . . ." Sully managed to get out, opening his mouth to speak . . . before—*promptly*—he felt a pair of invisible, frozen fingertips squeeze his lips back together.

The Horrox, as if nothing at all had occurred, continued,

"There is no difference. The only difference between Mortals and Creatures exists in your minds." The Horrox paused for a second and then raised a brutal smile. "In *our* minds."

Sully stood frozen, those ice-cold, invisible fingertips continuing to pinch his lips shut.

The Horrox went on, "But that shall all be taken care of . . . there are many changes coming, Sulliman, changes which shall affect not only Shellacnass, but the whole world; because—allow us to speak frankly—it seems that every Mortal on the face of the Earth has trouble accepting Creatures for who they are . . . and who have always been among them."

The Horrox stopped another moment, then fixed its gaze on something clear over Sully's head . . . something which Sully didn't turn to look at.

Finally, the Horrox snapped its attention back onto Sully.

"So," the Horrox said, "what do you say? Is the time right for change—is Shellacnass *ripe* for change?"

As Sully listened to the Horrox's voice echo about the throne room, he couldn't help but think on the question; find the inevitable answer that, *No, it wasn't* . . . and this—*merely thinking it in his thoughts*—proved enough for the Horrox to damn him.

The Horrox reached its arm out, pointed straight to Sully's chest.

Directly at his heart.

Sully felt a chill growing through his blood, passing through his veins.

As the world around him began to fade away—*again*—he felt several pairs of hands reach out to support him. To prevent him from tumbling down onto the dirt floor.

To prevent him from hurting himself.

37
———

BREAKING IN

ALTHOUGH FLUCKNOR was very much aware of the traitorous intricacies which surrounded this late-night, early-morning, breaking into *The Soore Whip*, he couldn't help but feel a scrap of delight burst through him to see Lou blast the lock clean off the back door of the pub.

For several seconds, Flucknor breathed in the scent of charred wood.

He felt the warmth of the hex carry through the air.

Bring the blood bulging up to his cheeks.

Lou slipped his hands, still glowing blue from the icy fire he had conjured, back inside his cloak sleeves.

Flucknor noted how Lou had busted through the lock almost soundlessly; he supposed that the only way anybody would have overheard the gentle, crackling sound was if they had been standing right behind them.

But they were alone here.

In the back alley of *The Soore Whip.*

Right away, Flucknor breathed in the stale odour of honey ale carrying on the draught; blowing out with the stifled pub air.

Just breathing in that odour sent his mind flailing, almost trundling off into another dimension, another time which'd existed before.

Happier times.

Times when he had understood and empathised with the Creatures' struggle.

A struggle which he *still* empathised with.

But not at any cost.

Flucknor crossed the threshold, staying close to Lou's boot heels, as if simply by keeping himself near to Lou would be enough for him to be protected.

Once Lou had taken maybe half a dozen steps into the back room of *The Soore Whip*, Flucknor watched on as the sword Lou had drawn and held down at his thigh was caught up with a neon-blue flame; running its way along the edge of the blade.

Flucknor wanted to stop.

He wanted to ask what they planned to do.

Surely—*surely*—they didn't mean to slaughter them in their beds.

Why hadn't Lou called upon the Royal Guards?

They could easily have taken the Creatures—the *Horrox* —prisoner.

Lou's sword—glowing with icy, blue magic—illuminated the gloom; it served to send the shadows scurrying for the corners.

Several times, from the effect of the shadows appearing and then retreating, Flucknor fooled himself that he saw rats skittering about the floor.

Rushing for the nooks and crannies.

But Flucknor knew, more than anything, that although Fhan—the proprietor of *The Soore Whip*—might not run the most stylish place in town; it was, at the very least, one of the cleanest . . . granted that *was* something of a dubious honour.

At first, Flucknor only heard quickened breathing.

That was what first drew his attention.

He watched on as Lou had already taken one—*or two*—steps too many into the darkness.

Into the unknown.

Flucknor supposed that he might've had the air in his lungs to call Lou back.

To warn him.

But the pub was so silent . . . a silence which seemed thicker than glass.

A silence which would be almost *profane* to break.

Acting quickly, trusting the prickle of ice magic and the indomitable urge which seized hold of him, Flucknor reached down for the handle of his dagger, protruding no more than a finger's width from its sheath.

He pulled his dagger free then whipped his arm back, feeling the weight of the dagger handle to be far heftier than he'd first imagined.

He hurled the dagger forward.

Everything seemed to slow down.

Flucknor observed his dagger duck and weave through the air; its blade tumbling over its handle as it went.

Right into the back of the little girl's head.

The little girl who'd appeared out of nowhere.

Out of the shadows.

Flucknor felt his heart tap hard at his ribs.

He had followed his *instincts*.

There had been no time to think . . . and he had been wrong . . .

The whole pub seemed to stand silent, stone-like in the gloom.

Flucknor shifted a glance at Lou, who had only just turned around.

To see the tiny body which lay at his feet.

Lying face down before him.

The dagger sticking out the back of the head.

Slowly, a gradual shift, Lou tilted his head upward so that his stare met with Flucknor's.

And for the first time—the first time *ever*—Flucknor saw fear in Lou's eyes.

But it wasn't fear of the situation.

Of what had just played out between them.

No, it was a fear of *Flucknor himself.*

As Flucknor continued to meet Lou's eye, his stare slowly dipped down, to the little girl's body which lay between them. And that was when Flucknor observed the body begin to change.

First it was the limbs, growing out from her legs.

And then her arms.

The rash-red skin of the Horrox.

Flucknor's heart continued to bob in his throat, and his whole body was rigid with tension.

But he could breathe again.

It hadn't been how he had imagined it.

He had merely done what Lou had asked of him.

He had killed one of the Horrox . . . one of the *Creatures.*

As if this knowledge had spread between the two of them, Lou turned his attention up the staircase, from where the Horrox—in its form of a Mortal girl—had emerged.

For a long series of moments, Flucknor was certain that Lou would simply turn and head up the stairs; that he would move them onto the next Creature to be killed.

But, instead, he finally spoke to Flucknor; in an even voice which told him, without mistake, that they were functioning on the level of equals.

"This was the reason I never told you anything," Lou said. "Why I never wanted to *corrupt* your alignment in the Magical Field . . . where you stand in relation to the Four Corners." He gestured vaguely at the body of the now-transformed Horrox at his feet. "And why I kept you close."

Lou turned to head back up the staircase.

But Flucknor couldn't allow Lou to simply say what he had without elaboration.

So Flucknor said, "Why *did* you keep me close?"

Gripping the banister of the staircase, his eyes flashing upward, to the next floor of the pub briefly, Lou aimed a sidelong glance at Flucknor once again. "So that you would know who's on your side—who's in your party . . . which are the ones you must protect."

Lou held Flucknor's gaze for another moment then he trod his way upstairs, and out of sight.

Flucknor remained standing still, in the darkness, for the longest time.

And he realised that he could shake the thought from his mind.

The thought of *just who* had decided which ones he must protect.

38

UNDERGROUND

SULLY COULD FEEL the delicious smells wafting all about him.

He breathed in the onions and the garlic, and he wondered, vaguely, how the Horrox had acquired such food out here, in the middle of the Winter's Moan.

Of course, he well knew that the Horrox shared Mortal tastes having lived among them for so long; that was well understood.

And it was a fact which he was *extremely* glad about right now.

He had two Horrox guarding him—one on each side.

They trod along at a business-like pace.

Their arms remained so straight down by their sides that it appeared they had invisible pins keeping them there.

Sully had no recollection of what had happened to him after he'd blacked out.

All he remembered was waking from a drowsy, seemingly long sleep five minutes ago.

And having this pair of Horrox—*not unkindly*—helping him up to his feet.

He had been at a kind of dead-end in the tunnel . . . other than that—other than the observation that he hadn't been in the Day'-gatarn's lair—there hadn't been anything he'd been able to recognise. Just more earth surrounding him. That scent of soil clinging to everything.

And the constant, soothing warmth.

As they had walked, one of the Horrox had spoken to Sully, told him that he would be given some hot food. And Sully had almost thanked the Horrox for speaking to him out loud, rather than inside his mind . . . he couldn't understand how the Horrox—or *any* Magical being—didn't go crazy from hearing voices within their own head.

Voices which weren't their own.

The pair of Horrox brought Sully through another doorway and into a kitchen.

There was a cooking area, seemingly built out of the earth.

A trio of Horrox stood about the stoves, working away with their wooden ladles at large, iron pots. The delicious-smelling liquid bubbled away within and Sully almost got neck ache from twisting to get a glance at the interior.

Off on the other side of the dug-out space, he saw there was a hole for steam to vent out. It was about big enough to stuff a turnip through. So, as a possible escape plan, it was a non-starter.

Sully turned back to the Horrox, waiting for their cue as to what he should do next.

They indicated that he should sit on one of the benches, which was—again—sculpted out of earth.

Sully did as he was told, and was glad to find that the mud of the bench was dried.

While he had been travelling out in the Winter's Moan, he had hardly been able to remember what it was like to find a dry seat to sit somewhere.

And now he could savour *that* particular pleasure.

The pair of Horrox who'd guided him here, to this kitchen, now stood their ground at the doorway. In the meantime, the Horrox acting as chefs, brought Sully over some clay bowls of the soup they'd been brewing up.

Although very glad to have the hot, buttery soup before him, Sully couldn't help but admit that he would've preferred it to arrive with something solid for him to chew on.

Sure enough, however, his request was granted.

The Horrox chefs brought over a freshly baked, warm-out-of-the-oven loaf of bread. One of them stayed behind to slice it up for Sully. When Sully glanced up at the Horrox who'd cut him the bread, he realised that he didn't care if this particular Horrox was male or female—*were they asexual Creatures?*—he was more than willing to plant a kiss of gratitude on that lizard-like snout.

Thankfully, though, it didn't seem necessary.

When Sully had got through with his soup, and a great deal of the loaf of bread, he turned his attention again to the doorway, noting the movement.

The Horrox—the one from the day before; the one from the throne room—appeared there.

Sully mimicked the other Horrox, as they stood up straight and proud, tilting their heads back ever so slightly while this Horrox passed between them.

When the Horrox reached him, it gave a wry smile and then sat down opposite.

Almost as if the Horrox acknowledged that it was imposing, it glanced down at the loaf of bread, and then, with a silent motion of its lips mimed, *May I?*

Sully, of course, gave the Horrox permission.

For several minutes, the two of them sat in complete silence.

Sully, all of a sudden, was aware of the quiet which'd drifted down over the rest of the kitchen.

While the kitchen hadn't been anything like a kerfuffle previously, there had at least been the odd *clang* of wooden spoon on iron pot, here or there . . . now, though, there wasn't so much as the drawing of breath.

Sully couldn't help but feel somewhat suffocated . . .

" 'Suffocate' you, do I?" the Horrox said.

Sully felt his whole body tense up.

He had forgotten that they could read minds.

The Horrox had heard everything he had just thought.

Unsure how to deal with this creeping knowledge, Sully blanked his mind and just stared back at the Horrox . . . *surely gawping . . .*

"Oh, I do apologise," the Horrox said. "The way I understand it, Mortal society frowns upon these *Magical* abilities. Not polite."

And then, as if to push this point, to deliberately make Sully uncomfortable, the Horrox followed up by speaking into Sully's mind again:

— *Such a shame do you not think?*

Sully, again, felt his heart skip a beat.

A chilly sensation creeped over his skin . . . the first time that he had felt anything like the cold down here in the Horrox's lair.

The Horrox gave a slight smirk as it chewed on the bread it held in its clawed fist. It swallowed quickly, and with a great display of strength from its throat muscles. "You know," it said, "you really *should* get to grips with our genders . . . I, for example, am *not* an 'it' but, rather, a *he.*"

"I . . ." Sully began, but realised he had nothing to say.

He was guilty within his own head.

"Allow me to introduce myself properly," the Horrox said. "My name is Arfklan, and I am the *King* of the Horrox, for want of a better term."

Sully wasn't sure what to make of this information.

He supposed that he was impressed, in some way, and in another way it allowed him to understand the behaviour of the other Horrox surrounding him.

"I never wished to live like my sons and daughters—I never *considered* it for me, a *Horrox*, to live as some sort of second-class citizen in Shellacnass." The Horrox paused for a long moment. "Although I'd be the first to admit that my race has had an *awful* lot of success at melding with Mortal societies; having infiltrated the power structures at *almost* every level."

Here, for some reason, Sully had the urge to speak up.

"Apart from the King," Sully said, and then he met the Horrox —*Arkflan's*—pit-black eyes.

Arfklan gave Sully a firm smile by way of response. "Quite right," he said. "But that can be corrected given time; and not just so that the Horrox shall govern in *Mortal* bodies; but they shall be allowed out into the open—magic shall no longer need to hide."

Sully felt his gut lurch and, all of a sudden, he wasn't convinced that the soup and bread had made him feel much better. His stomach had been near empty when he'd sat down.

Now he felt as if it might burst at the seams.

"All this, though," the Horrox went on, twizzling his fingers, "is beside the point."

Sully felt something twitch in his chest.

He wondered if the Horrox, as he had believed *him* to do earlier, had reached out an invisible hand to manipulate him.

"What I want to know is, where your companions are; where that *mage* and that *Glyph* are hiding out."

The Horrox fiddled with something in his robe before finally producing, from inside, a strange, button-sized object made of glass.

Sully couldn't help but lean forward.

Wanting to get a better look.

The glass was a sky-blue shade, but, when the Horrox passed his palm over the top of it, it quickly transformed to a pit-black.

And then the pain began.

All over Sully's body.

39

SPECULATION

FLUCKNOR STARED OUT through the window of his quarters, down into the streets of Ilsnare as they swept out from below. He eyed the hustle and bustle, the carts which weaved in and out of the pedestrians; a hive of activity.

If he was to open his window a little on the latch, and breathe in the air, he would smell the thick scent of fruits and vegetables, and then the freshly caught fish and cooking meat.

It was strange to think that his life had brought him here, to the urban centre of Shellacnass, when he had grown up so far away; back in the Sable Mountains.

He had been nothing but a simple village boy where the extent of his dreams and desires had been to possess his own strip of land . . . his own little cottage.

And to live out his dying days there.

But his magic wouldn't allow him.

Flucknor sensed stirring close by.

That was one of the effects of having paid his magic attention.

He had found, in the days following his and Lou's break-in at *The Soore Whip*, and all of those Horrox bodies they had left behind, that he was better able to sense magic when it was close by; it didn't matter whether it was ice or fire . . . he could just *sense* it.

As he did now.

Flucknor turned to the door, half expecting to see somebody staring in. But the door was kept firmly shut and he had to wait out the seconds before hearing the knock.

When he did, it made his gut squeeze in on itself.

Every time that he was given real-world confirmation of his magic's perceptive abilities, he felt the surprise afresh.

He asked for the knocker to come in and saw—right away—from the blue-white hair which sprouted from her scalp, that it was Gdandra.

Although he managed to raise a slight smile, the truth of the matter was that Flucknor felt somewhat flat inside. He felt as if he had done some great damage . . . and the truth of it, most likely, was that he had.

"Where would you like me to sit?" Gdandra said, her cheeks a little rosy, apparently from the exertion of climbing the Palace stairs. "Forgive me, but I'm getting a little old—I can't put the pressure onto the soles of my feet that I used to."

Flucknor indicated an armchair by the extinguished fireplace and, with a smile, she took up her place there. Even though Flucknor continued to stare out through the window, he could sense her watching him. To feel that his magic had become activated within his veins was almost as if he had discovered a third eye . . .

but one which floated about him, in all directions, and which knew no obstacle.

That was how Flucknor had sensed Gdandra out in the corridor.

Well, that *and* the fact that he had asked her here today.

They had many things to discuss and she had been clear with Flucknor that he was to contact her whenever something came up.

Whenever Flucknor wanted to know something about the magic which clawed through his body, and which would linger in him, like an infection, until the day he died.

Sometimes Flucknor found himself wondering what he had done to deserve this fate . . . if he had perhaps, in some previous life, offended the gods to such a degree that they had seen fit to punish him with magic in his veins.

Ice magic.

"So," Gdandra said, "what's bothering you?"

Flucknor felt the smile creep across his lips, not because of the question exactly, but the fact that Gdandra could see into his innermost thoughts; that she could read his dreams and memories as clearly as if she pictured them in her own head.

He knew this because she had attempted to teach him the same techniques, and of what Flucknor had witnessed so far, he could see that it was a potent tool indeed for any aspiring mage.

He hadn't yet managed to master the technique himself, and he knew that it would be many decades—if *that*—before he would be able to read another mage's thoughts . . . at least the thoughts of a mage stronger than he was; a mage like Lou.

Whenever Gdandra had willingly allowed Flucknor to experiment on reading her mind, he had found some surface-level sort of success. She would think of a word—and he would *read* it—or else she would think of an object—and he would *see* it.

But, whenever Flucknor attempted to dive deeper, he found it was like trying to swim through tar. It was impossible for him to sink below the surface without suffocating.

He recalled when he would pull out of her mind, and bring those watery, light-blue eyes back onto his that he would feel a sensation rippling across his skin akin to sunburn.

And he knew that behind her gentle smile there lurked an impossibly well-grounded defence. A resistance that Flucknor would never be able to break through . . . not while Gdandra still lived; there was simply too much for him to learn and not enough time.

So he could only *speculate* at her past.

Or he could ask her directly.

But, first, he turned his attention to the reason that he had called her here today.

Why he had felt that he required her counsel.

"Lou came to me," Flucknor said, shifting his gaze back onto hers. "In the middle of the night. He told me that he *knew* who had burned down the Great Hall."

"Oh?" Gdandra replied, her tone putting Flucknor in mind of a wizened teacher doing her best to praise the inquisitive nature of her young student without breaking out in wicked laughter at their naivety.

Flucknor kept on going, knowing that he couldn't stop. "We went to the place where I knew them to be hiding out—to the place which I'd reported to Lou as being their stronghold." He shook his head. "If only I'd known what he was planning . . .

perhaps I could've helped them . . . maybe they could've escaped . .
."

Gdandra cocked her head to one side. "Now," she said, "it's one
thing to walk in the light, but quite another to make full moral
judgements after the fact." She clasped her hands together in her
lap. "What makes you believe these Creatures didn't deserve to die?"

Flucknor glanced up at Gdandra, feeling that mock innocent
gaze of hers crossing his. He hadn't said anything about Creatures,
of course, and much less about the Horrox he had had a hand in
killing alongside Lou.

But, as Flucknor had already learned, spoken words were of
such miniscule importance to a mage that they almost held no rele-
vance at all.

What mattered—what *really* mattered—was what was held in
the mind.

And Gdandra could sift through Lou's thoughts at will.

All the same, Flucknor went through the motions of talking
out his thoughts.

"When Lou first came to me, I didn't know what he wanted me
to do; he just told me to go with him." Here Flucknor could do
nothing but shake his head. "When I got there, when we broke
into the location where these"—he knew there was no point in
concealing information; a pointless exercise if ever there was one
—"*Horrox* were hiding out, I felt that same urge I had back at the
Great Hall; that sensation that I needed to *do something* . . . that
there was something I could do to help out . . ."

There was a lull as Flucknor thought about how he would
utter the next words, and it was only when Gdandra broke in to
say, "Go on," that he managed to chain his thoughts back together.

"I had this urge," Flucknor said. "This deep, irrepressible urge within me to keep Lou safe."

Flucknor studied Gdandra for any emotion.

She remained stone-faced.

Giving nothing away.

Finally, apparently convinced that Flucknor was going to say nothing more, she said, "And what makes you think there was anything wrong with that urge?"

Flucknor thought to pick apart her use of the word 'wrong' only to realise that she had plucked it right out of his own mind.

He pushed that particular complaint away.

"From what Lou said," Flucknor replied. "How he suggested that he wanted it to be like this all along. That he wanted to develop me this way." It was here that Flucknor felt a flutter at the base of his chest and he couldn't help but turn on Gdandra with fresh suspicion. "About him wanting me to train under you—and only now. *Why*?" Flucknor said. "Why now?"

If Gdandra had something to hide, she showed no sign of making a conscious effort to do so . . . not that Flucknor could trust *that* particular observation.

"Lou," Flucknor said suddenly. "It was him—he was the one who burned the Great Hall down—who killed all but one member of the Council of Wisemen." He faced up to Gdandra. "Wasn't it?"

It seemed strange that Flucknor felt so calm, as if he was merely throwing around just another theory of magical craft . . . like one of the many meetings they had had through the weeks between the fire and the night-time raid on *The Soore Whip*.

Slowly, Gdandra rose up from the armchair.

She looked about herself, out of the window, then her eyes

finally lingered on Flucknor's. "You didn't kill all of the Horrox, did you? They weren't all present at *The Soore Whip* that evening."

Flucknor held himself still.

He felt a strong fear that Lou might be listening in from somewhere.

Finally, Flucknor replied, "No, they weren't all there."

Gdandra trod toward the door. "Well," she said, "there's your answer."

40

SEARCHING FOR A FUGITIVE

FLUCKNOR WAITED until darkness concealed everything.
Until the sun had gone down on the horizon.

Torchlight provided the only illumination.

Even knowing that Lou would be sealed away in the Throne Room—out of the way for the time being—Flucknor couldn't allow himself to relax.

On his way through the Palace corridors, he was convinced, at every corner, that Lou would emerge to block Flucknor's attempted escape.

The Royal Guards, of course, offered no sort of resistance to Flucknor. He *lived* in the Palace, after all. He was the High Representative; a role to which all citizens could relate and respect.

Once out on the streets of Ilsnare, after having kindly rejected the offers for a carriage to be called, Flucknor had no idea where he should go.

His intention had been a good one.

But he had nowhere to go.

He turned his mind to the music which leaked out of the taverns.

The *screech* of fiddles and the bellowing voices of drunkards.

Where would Brotsboore—the last remaining Horrox—be located now?

A little dizzily, Flucknor thought, of returning to *The Soore Whip*, as if Brotsboore would still be harboured there by the proprietor, Fhan.

Flucknor believed it a minor miracle that Fhan hadn't been at his tavern the night he and Lou had arrived at the back door . . . Flucknor had no doubt Lou would've killed Fhan without so much as blinking an eye; it was what Lou *believed* he had to do.

For what madness, Flucknor had no idea.

These past weeks, Flucknor had considered asking Lou straight out why they had done what they'd done, but he had lost his nerve. He was weary of stoking Lou's anger, of somehow bringing out the worst in the person who—*once upon a time*—he would've considered his best friend.

It was funny how things changed . . . no, *not funny* . . . terribly sad.

In the end, Flucknor settled on venturing to the Crystal Causeway marketplace.

From what he knew of the city—what *everyone* knew of the city—the merchants were among the most knowledgeable citizens. They saw everyone coming and going; and they missed *nothing*.

If there was an advantage to be had . . . a bit more grung to be squeezed, then *squeeze* it they did.

Their livelihoods depended on it.

Yes, that would be Flucknor's best chance.

When he arrived to the Crystal Causeway, everything was deserted. He didn't know what he had expected. Perhaps to see that there might be some merchants camped out on the streets; prepared to risk being thrown into the Gaols on vagrancy charges just so that they might nab one of the prime spots at first light.

Sometimes Flucknor forgot how well he had it.

How he *lived* in a Palace.

And before that it had been a mountain monastery.

Could he really have any complaints about his life?

In the end, after pacing up and down the Crystal Causeway twice, he spotted an illuminated window down one of the side streets.

Not seeing any other avenue for investigation, he made for it.

Only when he arrived beside the glass did he wonder to himself if this was the right thing to do . . . after all, how many citizens of Ilsnare would be receptive to a stranger knocking on their door in the early hours of the morning?

. . . Even if they were already awake . . .

Flucknor knocked anyway.

It would be a waste to have come all this way without really *trying.*

He waited patiently on the doorstep, listening to the scrabbling inside, the muttered voices. He wondered if he'd sent the occupants into an uncalled-for panic; if they believed it might be the Royal Guards.

Finally, the door opened up.

A man—with red hair and a thick beard; dark bags clinging to the bottoms of his eye sockets—peered out at Flucknor a touch blearily. He held the door open only a slit, and Flucknor imagined that the man must have his foot firmly pressed to the base of the door on the other side. "Yes?" he said.

Already, Flucknor felt an idiot for having knocked on the door; for having come out tonight at all . . . this whole idea had been half-baked and would serve only to arouse Lou's suspicions; and once Lou's suspicions were aroused there was no telling what he might do.

Might Lou see Flucknor as a traitor?

Was Flucknor a traitor?

But hadn't it been Lou who'd tried to turn Flucknor into his own personal guardian angel, and then exploited him?

If anybody was in the wrong, it was Lou.

Flucknor was sure about that.

He looked over the red-haired man and then tried out a smile. "I'm sorry to bother you at this time of night," he said, "but I was just wondering if you might've seen a friend of mine."

" 'A friend' ," the red-haired man echoed, "of yours?"

"That's right," Flucknor said.

There was a long pause while Flucknor wondered about filling in the gap.

But he decided it to be a waste of time.

The man would clearly have already judged him.

And why shouldn't he?

"My friend," Flucknor went on, "he wears a sable cloak, and he has, uh"—Flucknor wondered if Brotsboore was so convinced of his cause that he didn't so much as transform himself while out in public; while out walking in the street; Flucknor decided to make the leap of logic—"*red* skin?"

The red-haired man squinted long and hard at Flucknor, and he was convinced that he was on the brink of slamming the door in his face, before, with a look of revelation casting itself over his expression, he said, "Now you mention it there is this one person." He brought his fingers up to his mouth in thought—something which Flucknor considered a vaguely *childish* gesture. "See him walking along—going to the market some days."

Flucknor felt a weight lift up off his shoulders.

He forced himself to remain calm.

To get the information before he started into self-congratulation.

"Which way?" Flucknor got out, his tone hurried.

The red-haired man narrowed his eyes to slivers then cast his gaze from one direction of the lane to the other; and then he pointed off down the street. "That way," he said, and then, in an unprecedented move of confidence, he emerged from behind the door, stepped down into the street, and pointed. "That house— seen him coming and going from there."

Flucknor hardly thought to thank the man before he felt his feet moving from out beneath him, in the direction the man had indicated.

He eyed the door.

And was determined to get what he sought.

41

PAIN

THERE WAS NOTHING within Sully's body except for pain.

When the Horrox—*the King of the Horrox: Arfklan*—had revealed that button-like object, laid it on the bench between them; then turned its previously cheery sky-blue colour to pit-black with nothing but his palm, the pain had begun.

Sully felt the pain continue to wrack his body right now.

He had no idea where he might be located in the system of tunnels which made up the Horrox homestead. He was no longer in the kitchen, where he had met with Arfklan. He thought himself down one of the many tunnels . . . although this one was a dead-end.

He supposed that this was the way in which the Horrox could keep prisoners.

In constant pain.

It came in waves: overpowering, stinging his skin, cutting him down to the bone.

Never letting him rest.

Whenever the pain appeared to lessen, it proved only to be a false hope, because he would soon feel the same pain hundreds of times harder; hitting him with such force that he had to sink his teeth into his lower lip just to take his mind off the sensation.

In his more lucid moments, Sully had managed to glance up; to look about his surroundings. He thought he had seen other dead-end tunnels, with dozens of other prisoners all being kept down them . . . but, then again, he saw a lot of things.

Sully lay on the floor, after a particularly hard shock.

He looked upward; to the figures who towered over him.

Horrox.

What else would they be?

He wished them away, but wishing did no good; he knew that well enough now.

He had wished for the pain to stop so many times.

But it kept on coming.

This time, when the Horrox spoke to him—when Arfklan spoke to him—it was within his own mind. For the first time he could recall, Sully decided that he preferred this method of communication. The pain which he experienced was so sudden and so severe that he didn't trust himself not to bite clean through his tongue.

— *I am sorry for this, Sulliman, I truly am, but this is the best way for us to extract the location of your companions. I am afraid that we cannot trust the Mortal condition not to lie; a most troublesome thing* —honesty—*do you not think?*

Still feeling waves-upon-waves of pain passing through his

body, Sully wasn't in any sort of condition to begin discussing the intricacies of morals and ethics.

And yet, at the same time, he knew that what Arfklan said was true.

Even if he had had the faintest idea of how to find his companions there would have been little-to-no chance of him telling Arfklan.

Arfklan spoke into Sully's mind again:

— *Your mind, it really is most resistant. Of all the Mortal minds we have attempted to mine yours has been by far the most difficult to get to the bottom of.*

A fiercely sharp pain jabbed Sully right in his gut.

He groaned out loud, and then did something he never would've thought himself capable.

He replied to Arfklan in his own mind.

— *I ... do not ... know ... where ...*

The pain had been so sustained—and so *rhythmic*—that it had begun to affect Sully's thought patterns.

Arfklan spoke back to him:

— *This can all end if you tell us. Be a good little Mortal, okay?*

But Sully could only shake his head as he kneeled before them.

He could feel the tears of pain streaming down his cheeks. He had no means to stop them flowing. It was merely his body's knee-jerk reaction to extreme pain.

Sully managed to utter something else within his own mind.

— *I do not ... know.*

Arfklan replied to him:

— *Please, let us make this quick, shall we? Just tell me where they are and this all ends.*

Sully dizzily wondered if Arfklan meant the torture would stop.

Or if Sully would die.

At this point, Sully almost didn't care which.

He just wanted it to *stop*.

As Arfklan stood over him, he noticed something in the distance.

He could hear . . . no—*feel* something.

A distant, percussive *thump*.

Thump. Thump. Thump.

The pain paused for a long moment and Sully turned his attention upward, to Arfklan. He saw that Arfklan, too, had become distracted by the sound. It seemed that he uttered silent orders to the pair of Horrox who attended to him because they quickly scarpered in the direction of the ruckus.

When Arfklan turned his attention back to Sully, he gave him a slight smile. "Excuse me just a moment, wouldn't you?"

Sully watched on as the backs of Arkflan's heels disappeared around the corner of the tunnel.

As they passed out of sight.

There was a brief, wondrous moment when Sully dared to believe that the pain had stopped for good. That something had *happened* to stop it wracking his body.

But then it returned.

42

CRYSTAL CAUSEWAY AFTER DARK

A STEADY DRIZZLE was falling by the time Flucknor decided on what course of action he should take in approaching the house.

The house where—*apparently*—Brotsboore was to be found.

Flucknor eyed the front door, and then the windows which faced out into the street.

He had, of course, decided that it wouldn't be any strategy at all for him to just go and knock on the front door . . . to wait and see who would answer.

Brotsboore would be living in fear—that much Flucknor could take for granted.

Even if Brotsboore hadn't been there at *The Soore Whip* the night that Flucknor and Lou showed up to massacre the other Creatures, he would have learned of the attack.

Why else would he have fled here . . . to *this* place?

As Flucknor eyed the stone guttering which ran up to the

rooftop—and, more to the point, the *uncurtained* window there—
he realised that he could hear footsteps.

Thick and wet, and slapping against the cobblestones.

He turned to look.

There, standing at the top of the street, was a figure in a sable
cloak.

All the breath left his lungs.

Suddenly, he couldn't think of a thing to say or do.

His mind went blank.

He wondered if Brotsboore might slip a slender, red-skinned
wrist out through the sleeve of his cloak and cast a hex on him . . .
perhaps make it so that his own blood drowned him alive.

Maybe that would be a just end for him; a just punishment for
the wicked deeds which he had committed on Lou's behest.

If Brotsboore had wanted Flucknor dead then he would have
performed a killing curse already.

But he was holding off, waiting . . . for what?

As Flucknor tried his best to peel back the shadow which lay
over the face of the hooded figure, he noticed something peculiar.

At first it was nothing more than a skitter through his blood.

A ticklish, itchy sensation.

But then it became more profound.

Harder for Flucknor to ignore.

So similar to the sensation which'd struck him back at the
Great Hall—when he had taken it upon himself to rush on into
the burning building and save whoever he could.

Working on instinct now, Flucknor took a step toward the
cloaked figure.

He felt the ice magic itching through his veins.

He tried to recall any appropriate advice that Gdandra

might've given him for a situation like this, but he couldn't bring to mind anything at all.

And yet he continued to approach the cloaked figure.

More steps.

Closing the gap.

Still no hex—*no curse*—flew from Brotsboore's fingertips.

Perhaps Flucknor had got this all wrong; perhaps he had read the situation incorrectly . . . had they somehow done Brotsboore a favour by slaying all of the Horrox; all those who had shared their lodgings at *The Soore Whip?*

Flucknor had no idea.

Could he do anything except ask?

When Flucknor cleared his throat to speak, he felt his heart hammering in his chest.

At the same time, Flucknor did recall something Gdandra had instructed him.

How to sense magic.

Or, more to the point, how he should *pay attention* when magic surrounded him.

And, right now, Flucknor could sense nothing at all.

Was it because he was stressed?

Had his natural capabilities been dulled by the situation itself?

. . . Or was there some other explanation?

He thought back to *The Soore Whip* and how he had sensed magic flowing all around him; the magic which ran through the veins of the Horrox hiding out there. It'd been almost like a rush of blood to the head; a feeling that'd been impossible to ignore.

But Flucknor could sense nothing at all now.

He wondered if the Horrox—if *Brotsboore*—was casting some

sort of an enchantment, so that he would keep his magic a secret from wandering minds.

Or maybe there was some other explanation.

It was only when Flucknor took another step toward the cloaked figure that he realised he had been wrong the whole time.

In the torchlight which flickered about the streets, Flucknor caught a glimpse of the face held in shadow by the hood. And he saw that it wasn't Brotsboore . . . not at all.

For a couple of seconds, he found himself staring at the thick, full lips; catching the slight sheen of the reflection which laced them. And then his attention moved upward, to that single eyeball which occupied the middle of the face.

The one which considered Flucknor now.

It was a *Cyclops*.

And then Flucknor thought of his name:

Rintersyart.

Another of the Creatures who had hidden out at *The Soore Whip*.

Another who had survived the slaughter.

It was with a thin, reedy voice that Rintersyart spoke to him.

"Are you alone?"

"Yes," Flucknor replied, without thinking.

Rintersyart turned his back to Flucknor, and began to tread across the cobblestones. "Follow me," he said. "Brotsboore has been expecting you."

43

TIME FOR ACTION

A S THE CYCLOPS, Rintersyart, led him through the tangled back streets—further and further away from the Crystal Causeway—Flucknor imagined that, at any given second, Brotsboore and a group of rejuvenated other Horrox he had gathered, would leap from the shadows; all of them ready and willing to slice his throat.

Why wouldn't they?

This was the perfect opportunity.

Flucknor had come alone.

He had even admitted as much to Rintersyart.

They might avenge those who Flucknor and Lou had put to death.

But nobody emerged from the shadows of the side streets, and Flucknor felt the anxiety tighten across his chest; send his heart beating harder and harder against his ribs.

Finally, after what must have been ten, fifteen minutes of walking, Rintersyart brought them to a halt down an unsuspecting side alley. When Flucknor looked to Rintersyart, he saw that a slight smile lingered on his lips.

"None of the others were certain," Rintersyart said. "None of them really *believed* that you would come here; that you would face up to Brotsboore . . . but *I* did . . ."

There were more of them, then; that much could be implied from Rintersyart's comments.

Flucknor's stomach muscles twisted on the leg of lamb he'd chomped down earlier that evening.

Perhaps they wanted him to know exactly *why* he would be put to death before they actually turned on him and did it.

Flucknor stayed quiet as Rintersyart fiddled with the lock on the door, and then, finally, pushed it open to allow Flucknor to pass through.

When Flucknor crossed the threshold, he breathed in the strong scent of lemons—that sharp, *citric* scent which clung to the air. The smell was so pronounced, so impossible not to feel tingling and *biting* at the back of his throat, that he was certain Rintersyart would turn and provide him some sort of explanation.

Surely, if the plan was for Flucknor to tread directly into the midst of his own death then Rintersyart would want to do whatever he could to make Flucknor feel at home.

To make Flucknor believe that there was nothing at all to fear.

Rintersyart simply closed the door behind them, and then led the way along the corridor.

Flucknor paused. He looked back over his shoulder, knowing this was his final chance to escape the building; that he could simply slip back out into the night.

Disappear.

If he cried out loud enough, he knew that a good dozen or so Royal Guards would come running to see what the trouble was.

But Flucknor watched on as, up ahead, Rintersyart turned the corner and slipped from sight; going deeper into the house.

He breathed to the very bottoms of his lungs. He could feel the tingle of ice through his veins.

What it was telling him, he couldn't quite be certain . . . but something buried into his lower consciousness implored him to follow Rintersyart; if only to see for himself that it was true; that not all the Horrox involved with Brotsboore had been killed that night in *The Soore Whip.*

The zesty scent of the lemons only grew stronger and stronger as Flucknor put one foot in front of the other, progressing into the building. He noted the wood panelling on the walls. He felt the dusty, full air press up against his skin.

Everything about this place spoke claustrophobia to him.

And yet he proceeded.

Feeling that he could do nothing else.

When he noted the orange glow up ahead, spilling out through the doorway and onto the wooden floorboards, he felt a twitch through his heart.

Another warning?

A *final* warning?

From what he had understood from his lessons with Gdandra so far, he was aligned with the light. He was skewed toward protecting others . . . to keeping others from harm.

But he had never thought to ask the question of whether there might be some facet of his alignment which was reserved for protecting *himself.*

But he kept on going.

One foot in front of the other.

Until he stepped through the doorway.

Into a room smothered in shadows, despite the torch which blazed above.

The Horrox—*all* Creatures—used a magic far subtler than that found in Mortal veins.

It was powerful and bound up with their very being.

From what Flucknor understood of Creatures' magic, there was none of the struggle to understand that which flowed through them; no struggle for them to *control* . . . it was more like the simplicity of using a limb one was born with.

Sometimes Flucknor wondered if it was possible to even scratch the surface of comprehension in terms of the magic which Creatures possessed and utilised.

As Flucknor turned on the spot, he sensed figures all around him, seated on chairs; all of them with their eyes fixed onto him. A prickling sensation passed over the surface of his skin.

Once again, as had happened when he'd been snatched from the street, he heard the voice in his head. Brotsboore's voice:

— *You are a brave man to come here tonight. To risk your life.*

Flucknor felt his body lock up, but his mind remained nimble as he spoke back to Brotsboore within his own mind:

— *I wanted to ask you a question.*

— *A 'question'?*

Flucknor glanced about himself, then decided he should get on with his asking:

— *I want to know the truth. Whether or not you were the ones who burned down the Great Hall.*

There was a long silence within Flucknor's very mind, and he felt himself almost slipping away from the room; as if the soles of his feet might become so heavy as to cause him to sink down into the floor . . . *down* into the ground.

Perhaps what Flucknor perceived was his oncoming death.

Arriving steady and sure; at a plodding pace.

Finally, from among the cloaked figures all sitting on their chairs, Flucknor took stock of one of them leaning forward; hands still firmly clasped to their kneecaps. And he listened to the familiar, throaty—*rasping*—voice, spoken aloud and sourced from the shadow of the hood.

"Do you really believe us such monsters, Flucknor? Do you believe that only in Creatures there can exist an evil so pronounced?"

Flucknor met with the shadow beneath the hood, and he wondered if he was staring directly into Brotsboore's pit-black eyes.

Slowly, Brotsboore reached up, and then brought his hood down to his shoulders.

He exposed his face.

The lizard-like snout.

Red skin.

The scabs covering his scalp.

And, of course, the pit-black eyes.

It was only when Flucknor turned his attention to the scar which ran from his left cheek, and then all the way down to the corner of Brotsboore's mouth, that he recalled how he had struck out with the dagger . . . when the Horrox had snatched him off the street.

When he spoke again, Flucknor noticed that the other dozens of figures who had previously surrounded Brotsboore were no longer there. That they had—*apparently*—just vanished into midair. Brotsboore's voice seemed to carry less weight this time; it retained its raspy quality but had lost a great deal of its power.

"Answer my question," Brotsboore said. "Do you believe that such evil as that which burned down the Great Hall could only have come from unfeeling Creatures?"

"No," Flucknor replied. "No, I don't."

Feeling as if somebody was still watching him, he turned around quickly, then looked to the door.

He saw Rintersyart was standing there, his own hood having fallen down to his shoulders.

His Cyclops's eye was laid bare in the torchlight.

"We're all that's left now, Flucknor," Rintersyart said. "It's up to us to decide whether we escape the city before more force—more of these accusations—head our way."

Flucknor held Rintersyart's single eye for a long while, and then he turned back to Brotsboore. "It was Lou who burned down the Great Hall, then, wasn't it?"

Brotsboore remained still, seeming far smaller than Flucknor could ever remember.

And then, with an almost undiscernible movement, he gave a doleful nod.

44

BREACHED

W HEN SULLY NOTICED that the constant pain which'd jangled his body for what seemed like weeks or months had stopped, he could hardly draw breath.

All the air seemed to have deserted his lungs.

He felt his bones throbbing, as if they expected another onslaught to follow at any moment. He was on a constant state of alert, prepared to channel every last scrap of remaining energy in his body into combatting the pain; into trying to retain his own thoughts.

To keep himself sane.

Sully knew this was the Horrox's tactic, that they hoped to break down his defences by way of constant bombardment of his mind . . . to make it so that he could no longer resist their attempts to discover the locations of the Glyph and Syre.

He supposed that they would rather kill him and be *sure* that he didn't know of their locations than leave him alive and allow for any sort of doubt.

And Sully didn't want to die.

Not here—not *underground* . . . like a corpse already buried.

On his hands and knees, Sully reached out. He felt for the soil beneath him, and he worked to keep himself upright. His heart beat so hard that he could feel each of its pounds in his throat, and all through every one of his aching bones.

He glanced up, sure that he would see the smirking, self-satisfied face of Arfklan staring back at him, that button of his lying flat on his palm; no doubt enjoying the sight of Sully believing himself to have been spared his torture . . . the colour of the button having returned to its neutral sky-blue tone.

And then, swiftly, without warning, the *black* would return.

But there was nobody ahead of Sully.

Nobody accompanied him.

And he was blissfully glad.

Trembling all over, Sully helped himself up to his feet.

He reached out and supported himself with the wall of the tunnel, feeling the cool surface of the tightly packed soil between his fingers.

When he tried to take a step, he nearly fell forward and landed flat on his face.

But he just managed to catch himself in time.

It was a struggle to keep putting one foot in front of the other, and to keep his eyes fixed on the corridor which ran past the dead-end he had emerged from.

Torchlight flickered, beating back the darkness.

Only when Sully reached the opening which led back into the

tunnel did he notice the *thump, thump, thump* from before. And his mind turned to the Day'gatarn.

In the distance, he was sure that he heard a *roar* . . . or was it just his imagination?

For several seconds, as Sully glanced about him, into the deserted tunnels, he was certain that this was some sort of a dream . . . a *delusion* perhaps . . . perhaps the pain had simply reached its zenith, got to a point which his mind could no longer tolerate and it had shown him mercy; allowed him to escape into the realms of his subconscious imaginings.

He turned around.

He looked back to where he had been.

The dead-end tunnel which'd served as his prison.

He could see where he had lain, the marks from his body-weight, and where, in one fit of particularly tormenting pain, he had scrabbled against the mud floor and dug out holes for his elbows and knees so that he might hold himself still.

Anchor himself.

The trembling subsided slightly. Enough so that Sully could see straight.

That he could look along the dug-out corridor.

Nobody was here.

Where had the Horrox gone?

In his mind, he pictured their red skin, and their lizard-like snouts.

The ever-present ambivalent expression sketched across their features.

Once again, Sully heard the *roar* reverberate through the subterranean corridors and he felt a twitch of anticipation pass over the surface of his skin.

What was he supposed to do?

Should he run?

And if he *did* run then where would be run *to*?

It only took another round of the *thump-thump-thumps* to make Sully's mind up; that it didn't matter where he ran. That he would be safer anywhere else than where he was right now . . . at a dead-end.

So he picked a direction—it didn't matter which—and set off running.

45

UNITED

FLUCKNOR GAZED OUT over the dawning day.

He watched on as the golden light caught the glass rooftops of the buildings of Ilsnare.

In the distance, beyond the Crystal Causeway, he made out Ilsnare Palace and he wondered if Lou had already realised he was gone; that he had snuck out of his bed in the middle of the night and gone strolling through the city.

Looking for Creatures.

Flucknor recalled when he had first arrived to the Crystal City. It had been overwhelming. So many people. Seeing all of them at once. The hustle and bustle as everybody pushed to get through the streets. And how nobody seemed to look anybody else in the eye.

For many weeks, following his arrival, Flucknor had been unable to comprehend how people could live so naturally under

such conditions, and yet, at the same time, he found himself intox-
icated by the idea. Unable to resist the *rattle* and *hum* of the place.

Now, though, he felt that the city had something truly poiso-
nous flowing through its veins. Something which could only be
quenched through the deposing of Louson Dorf as king . . . the
'*Hitchking*', as many gossiping citizens termed him.

Flucknor wondered at the attack which Tineoots—*the butler*—
had launched on Lou; and how he had been appalled by the idea
at the time . . . almost as appalled as he had felt when Lou had
decided to cast Syre, his own sister, into exile.

Of course, though, Syre was so much more to Flucknor than
simply Lou's sister.

She had been his lover.

And—*even now*—he longed to be with her.

Was it worth running the risk of death to try?

The night before, Brotsboore had accepted Flucknor back
among their dwindling group of rebels; a group which now only
counted Brotsboore and Rintersyart among its numbers.

The rest had been killed by Lou in the raid on *The Soore Whip*.

Flucknor was still reeling from this decision, wondering what
it might mean.

He would need to leave his role as High Representative
behind, of course; and although this seemed a somewhat obvious
observation, he couldn't help but feel a slightly nauseous feeling
twirling away in his gut at the prospect.

He had spent time and energy growing used to the role; to how
he might be able to easily slip between the King and the Council
of Wisemen, offering guidance where it might be required. And
there were, also, the words which Gdandra had given him.

The ones which he'd never forget.

About how he was the right choice as High Representative.

Only now did Flucknor see how wrong she had been . . . in what world did Gdandra believe that Flucknor was the right person to act as a sort of 'guardian angel' for a soulless murderer?

And on what basis should Flucknor live his life only to be a glorified shield for Louson Dorf?

Flucknor now understood why Lou had prohibited him from leaving the city on pain of imprisonment; Lou was struck into terror by the idea that his guardian angel might flutter away and never come back. That he would lose the protection he had worked so hard—*and for so many years*—to achieve.

When Flucknor turned his head, he saw that Brotsboore and Rintersyart stood in the doorway.

And that the two of them were looking beyond him—out through the window—watching on as the day dawned.

It was Brotsboore who spoke.

"We're leaving the city—*tonight*," he said.

Flucknor took a moment to absorb these words, almost like a blow to his solar plexus.

Then he looked up. He felt Brotsboore's inky, black eyes lingering.

Rintersyart's single, looming eye fully concentrating on him.

Flucknor knew precisely what this was.

A call to arms.

This was to be Flucknor's final chance to show his dedication to the cause; to the cause of justice and equality for all Creatures throughout Ilsnare, and Shellacnass.

One day . . . *one more day* . . . that was all Flucknor had.

All the time he had to say goodbye to Ilsnare.

And he had so much to do.

46

FAREWELL

FLUCKNOR REACHED the Borronder District a little after the sun beamed down with full strength on the streets of Ilsnare. As he had caught the horse-drawn carriage and been driven to Gdandra's apartment, he had become paranoid that Lou's network of Spies—*the Eye*: a network of which Flucknor had once been a part—might have been given orders to track his every movement.

Although Flucknor was beyond worrying for himself—he had decided that if Lou did decide to imprison him then it was preferable to being asked to continue his current role as High Representative; and Royally Appointed Guardian Angel—he was concerned that the Eye might've noted the location of Brotsboore and Rintersyart.

Flucknor couldn't face any more death.

Being *responsible* for any more death.

As he passed in through the doorway, having been told to

come inside, he felt himself nearly gagging from the strength of the lavender perfume. He wondered if this was a ruse, if Gdandra had sensed that he was on his way here . . . although what purpose smothering Flucknor with perfume might serve sent his mind skittering.

He found Gdandra crouching down over the fireplace, removing a kettle of boiling water from within; and, apparently, on the cusp of making a pot of tea.

Today she was wearing a floaty, rose-white summer dress. Her wispy, white-blue hair was contained in the form of a bun around the back of her head. She glanced up at him briefly, her watery-blue eyes meeting with his own.

Just as Flucknor had suspected, she didn't look surprised to see him.

"Take a seat," she said, turning back to the kettle. "The tea will just be a minute."

Flucknor sat in one of the armchairs and then gazed out across the rooftops of the surrounding apartments. He saw that some women had emerged with their arms full of laundry, and that they were setting about hanging them to dry on the flimsy ropes strung up from one side of the rooftop to the other.

He supposed that they had just finished washing up the breakfast crockery and that they'd graduated to their next task about the house.

Sometimes he wondered how much simpler life would be as a housewife.

No magic. No drama.

No *excitement*?

On balance, Flucknor believed that he could live just fine without the excitement.

Not that he had much of a choice now.

Seeing no reason to dance around the point, he turned his attention to Gdandra, who was now pouring out the boiling water into a teapot, and he said, "I'm leaving the city tonight."

Gdandra didn't reply right away, and Flucknor was surprised to see the slight smile break out on her lips, as if there was something amusing about the situation.

If there *was* something amusing about the situation then Flucknor would've very much liked to have heard it . . . he could've done with a good chuckle.

"Well, then," she said. "I suppose you've given the matter a good deal of thought."

"Louson Dorf set the fire," Flucknor replied. "In the Great Hall."

Gdandra formed an 'oh' shape with her mouth, but, somehow, Flucknor didn't quite believe this gesture totally sincere.

Flucknor went on, "As I told you before, I'm not happy with being his guardian angel; not without him having so much as *asked* me . . . it's better that I leave him to whatever schemes he has planned for Ilsnare. I won't be able to fully commit to them."

Gdandra set the kettle, still spewing steam, back down on the hearth. She wiped her damp hands on the sides of her apron, and then arched an eyebrow. "I suppose you've notified the King of your plans?"

Flucknor felt a tingle pass through his blood.

When Gdandra set her eyes onto his, he became more uncomfortable still.

The itching beneath the surface of his skin became so unbearable that he had to rise up out of the armchair and tread over to the window.

He breathed in the city air, and took in the thick smoke from the kilns and blacksmiths and all those other outlets. He could still recall the fresh mountain air of the village where he had grown up; Dweldwock...

Apart from anything else, he could hear—*loud and clear*—the call of his past ringing in his ears.

He knew that his time in the Crystal City was coming to an end.

Did he wish to *die* here?

...No, not if he could help it...

"Here," Gdandra said, appearing at his side and handing him a cup of tea.

Flucknor glanced down into the dark, purple-coloured liquid. He watched it swirling slightly from where Gdandra had stirred in a spoonful of sugar.

Already he breathed in the thick scent of berries which plumed up from within and he felt his mind casting him back to the mountains once more.

To those lush, swishing grasses.

The gentle breeze blowing against his cheeks.

And his heart beating full and steady.

No knowledge of magic... no knowledge of Louson Dorf... or the Crystal City.

He turned his attention back to Gdandra.

Took in her gaze once more.

"I can't go to Lou," Flucknor said. "He already told me what he will do if I try to leave the city—if I try to escape from him."

Gdandra eyed him steadily for several seconds, peering over the rim of her cup of tea. "You haven't even *tried* to explain?"

Flucknor shook his head. "And I have no intention of doing so

—I can't put the lives of the others in danger . . . they can't come to more harm because of *me.*"

There was a profound silence between them, and, out of the window, Flucknor heard a thick *slap-slap-slap* of one of the house-wives beating some damp garment; squeezing all the moisture from it.

Gdandra was the one to break the silence. "I think you should speak with him, before you go. You might be surprised about what he has to say."

Flucknor thought about this for a moment, and then, acting spontaneously, he set his mug down, stood up from his chair and embraced her.

Despite her apparently excellent mind-reading prowess, she seemed just as taken aback by this development as Flucknor himself was.

As he embraced her delicate body, he peered into the embers of the dying kitchen fire, and he thought about how sad he would be to leave Gdandra behind—with all that she still had left to teach . . . already she had illuminated so much of the path.

47

CERTAIN DEATH

S ULLY KEPT ON running through the endless underground tunnels, taking in only the fact that one was more alike than the previous one.

Down several of the tunnels, he spotted other prisoners; all of them Horrox from what he could tell. And he realised that he must've been one of the first to break free of the pain which'd been inflicted on him . . . the Horrox prisoners were still coming around slowly, blinking away the daze which'd set in from the overwhelming pain.

Sully's whole body still tingled. His heart skipped along without giving him so much as a single second's respite.

Torchlight flickered all around him—more than anything making him dizzy.

He wanted to slump down, press his back up against the wall, and fall into a deep and well-deserved sleep.

But he still had a way to go yet.

Before he was out of danger.

As Sully bounded along he couldn't shake the feeling that he was only getting closer and closer to the sound of the *thumping* footsteps; and to the sound of the *roar*.

But what was he supposed to do?

He could hardly turn around and go back the way he'd come .. . that, he knew, would lead him into a dead-end.

When Sully turned the corner, he felt one of the *thumps* harder than any that had come before, and he was forced to dive into the tunnel wall to keep himself from tumbling head over heel.

Sully caught his breath, leaning up against the wall. He could feel the vibrations of the footsteps of the beast—*the Day'gatarn*— still bounding about up ahead.

In an act of desperation, he wildly wondered if he might be able to excavate his way out of the tunnel with his bare hands. He jabbed his index finger into the wall by way of example, and wasn't entirely surprised when it bounced back off the hardened, packed soil.

Sully held himself still.

Pressing his back against the wall.

Trying to get his heartbeat back under control.

He was certain that the footsteps were getting louder; even as he stood where he was.

And he knew that the only explanation was that the Day'- gatarn was approaching.

That it would soon be upon him.

When Sully tried to move his legs, he felt as if his muscles had been frozen by invisible hands. He glanced about; sure that it must be Arfklan—*the Horrox King*—who was to blame; but, in the end, he realised that there was nobody there except for himself.

He was alone.

And about to do battle alone.

As he tensed up his entire body, ready to feel the Day'gatarn's ripping claws—or talons, whatever it was that the beast possessed —he mumbled a prayer under his breath to any gods who might be listening . . . and ones who had such good hearing that they could listen in on thoughts as they whizzed through a mind *miles* underground.

He felt the footsteps getting closer still.

The air temperature shifted slightly.

And the strong smell of Mortal feet returned.

This was it . . . Sully was sure . . . he felt as if his body would be torn apart in a matter of seconds.

He closed his eyes in anticipation.

And listened into the sounds of heavy breathing.

The *damned* Creature towering over him.

He hoped this would be quick.

Quicker than the pain inflicted on him by Arfklan.

Right as Sully was sure that the beast would strike him, he heard a familiar voice.

Syre's voice.

"Don't just stand there! Hop on!"

Sully couldn't quite believe it until he opened his eyes.

And even then, to see the Creature before him; its ruffled *feathers* stained with blood . . . its sharp *beak* fit for slicing through skin . . . he almost felt himself faint again; and he might well have done if it hadn't been for Syre's sure grasp; taking hold of him with invisible arms, hundreds of times stronger than her own, and lifting him up so that he sat behind her on the Day'gatarn's back.

Sully turned to see the Glyph mounted behind him.

"Hi," it said, out loud, and with its voice leaping a touch as it did so. "Sorry about the delay."

Sully gripped tightly to the beast's flanks and turned to face the direction of travel.

48

ESCAPE

FLUCKNOR THOUGHT he would've felt more nerves at the prospect of defying Lou; of leaving Ilsnare behind for good. But he was surprised, as he glanced back over the faces of Brotsboore and Rintersyart, that he felt sturdy and could stand still without effort . . . without so much as his hands shaking.

He wondered where this—surely misplaced—sense of confidence might've come from.

He decided that it could rightly be due to the adrenalin which rushed through his veins, and which didn't allow him so much as a single conscious thought.

All he could focus on was the City Gates, and how he, Brotsboore and Rintersyart would pass through them . . . or, as they had planned it themselves, how they would pass *under* them.

Throughout his many years in Ilsnare, Flucknor had often heard the rumours about the Catacombs which ran beneath the cobbled streets of the city. And that the Catacombs, in turn, offered a whole myriad of exit points from the Crystal City.

Flucknor himself knew of only one way to enter the Catacombs.

It was located in Ilsnare Palace.

And there lay the trouble.

Flucknor had spent a long while earlier that day—in the afternoon, soon after he had returned from Gdandra's home—mentally *screaming* at Brotsboore and Rintersyart, unwilling to believe the truth they told him. That the two of them, a pair entwined with all manner of unscrupulous activities in the Crystal City, knew *nothing at all* of these secret entrances into—and exits *out of*—the city.

From what Flucknor gathered, from what Brotsboore and Rintersyart had informed him, most of the types of people who held the secrets to the locations of the entrances and exits to the Catacombs around the city kept those secrets held very tightly indeed.

It was a cold fact that those who betrayed the locations of the entry points to the Catacombs would soon find that two things came to pass:

One was the death of the one who'd betrayed the secret.

The second was that the Royal Guards would converge on the entrance to the Catacombs and seal it off to prevent any further voyages into its depths.

Flucknor hoped that the same fate hadn't befallen the entrance he knew about at Ilsnare Palace . . . because then they really would be trapped.

Already, Flucknor felt his mind spinning at the prospect of returning to the Palace.

He had almost shut a mental door on that aspect of his life, determined to move on from everything it had represented to him … to think that he would now have to return was somewhat horrifying—not to mention the fact that he would be putting both Brotsboore and Rintersyart into perilous danger.

Something which he had hoped to avoid by his own departure from Ilsnare.

Flucknor had examined the issue from all angles and the only solution that he had been able to produce was the three of them sneaking into the Palace; getting into the Catacombs through the entrance he knew about.

For them to waste time going about town, attempting to track down someone who might be able to show an entrance to a bunch of strangers clearly carried far too great a danger.

And not to mention the fact that they hadn't much money to spare; and the money that they did have would be better put to work once they managed to escape the Crystal City.

If they managed to escape the Crystal City …

No, no matter how their discussions progressed, Flucknor could see no other way of them getting away from Ilsnare other than through the Palace entrance to the Catacombs.

With this matter decided, Flucknor turned to Brotsboore and Rintersyart and gave them each a hardy smile. "I suppose we could wait until later but it's dark now—there's no better time for us to go if this is what we want."

Neither of them replied.

49

THE PALACE LIBRARY

F LUCKNOR COULD FEEL the darkness closing in on him when he reached the Palace Gates; Brotsboore and Rinter-syart behind him.

The Royal Guards said nothing at all to Flucknor as he passed them by, and why should they?

He was the High Representative, after all, and following the deaths of the Council of Wisemen in the fire at the Great Hall, his role had taken on considerably more responsibility.

That aside, he was the closest friend the King had.

What reason would they have to stop him?

As Flucknor slipped by the Guards, he knew they had all the reason in the world to demand that he—and the companions who trailed in his wake—stop right away.

Flucknor was going directly against the King's will . . . he was going against that which the King had prohibited. And, what was more, he was bringing these two Creatures along with him.

Flucknor acted quickly once he was inside the Palace; he had no intention of lingering any longer than was strictly necessary.

He led Brotsboore and Rintersyart through the corridors; in the direction of the Palace Library, where he believed the entrance to the Catacombs to be located.

Flucknor had been sure of the location of the entrance . . . now, though, he couldn't help but feel doubts creeping in. He hadn't ever *personally* explored, of course.

For some reason, he had simply never felt the curiosity.

Once again, Flucknor cursed Lou for having exiled Syre from Ilsnare, because he was certain that she would've long ago sought out the entrance to the Catacombs.

She would've known *exactly* where to go.

As it was, Flucknor led the pair of cloaked figures into the Library, and they all breathed in the air; thick with aged leather book bindings.

And, of course, Flucknor's old enemy:

Dust.

The bookshelves were the tone and colour of walnut shells and the spines of the books were stuffed into place, having obviously, in the long and grand history of the Palace, had great use.

Flucknor turned his attention upward, as he could never help but do whenever he entered the Library. He examined the glorious, glass dome above their heads; much like the one in the Throne Room. The stars twinkled down on them, tiny spots of bright-white light.

He could also make out the sallow glow of the moon.

At this time, the light from the moon and stars was all that illuminated their path.

He had made it clear to both Brotsboore and Rintersyart that neither of them was to use their magic to bring light to bear on their surroundings until they were well sunken; down in the Catacombs. If either of them attempted to use their magic before then, there would be a strong possibility of Lou sensing their presence.

Then again, Flucknor supposed Lou might already have sensed them.

After all, Lou's magical powers were far in advance of Flucknor's own.

A slight chill ran through Flucknor's heart to think of what he was about to do—about what he, Brotsboore and Rintersyart were going to do.

Turning his mind back to the task, Flucknor jerked his head around to the large, stone engraving on the eastern wall of the Library. He had always found it striking, right from the first time when he had set foot in this place . . . then again, he supposed it was difficult *not* to be struck by it; occupying the entirety of a wall as it did.

The stone engraving was of a mounted archer, in the saddle of a rearing horse.

The archer himself, as Flucknor often wryly observed, was stripped to the waist so that he might expose the well-toned abdomen. He was firing off at some unseen target, beyond the remit of the etching itself.

Flucknor turned his attention back over his shoulder—to Brotsboore and to Rintersyart—the two of them following on his heels.

He spoke directly into their minds so as not to alert any nearby Royal Guards who might be strolling along the corridors.

— *This is the place. Give me a hand.*

Brotsboore and Rintersyart, almost as if they had rehearsed

exactly what would be required of them, moved into place at either side of the stonework etching.

One of them to either side of its bulk.

Flucknor took up a position crouched down, at the base of the stone.

And then, with a silent count which only Flucknor, Brotsboore and Rintersyart could hear, they all brought the full force of their muscles to bear.

Flucknor felt its enormous weight shifting.

Ever so slightly at first.

But *shifting.*

As Flucknor edged his fingertips further into the crack at the base of the stone, he prepared himself to put a fresh effort into dragging it free.

And it was then that he felt the cold—*burning*—heat rip through the air.

A neon-blue bundle of light flashed overhead.

It careened into the wall and brought rock tumbling down from above.

Right on top of them.

50

THE WINTER'S MOAN

SULLY'S ENTIRE BODY seemed to be overheating and freezing to death.

All at once.

He felt the strange, otherworldly, body warmth from the Day'-gatarn as he squeezed its feathered flanks between his thighs. The harsh, chilling breath of the Winter's Moan blew hard against Sully.

Almost as if the wind itself tried to force him tumbling down.

To land with a sickening *crunch* on the hard-packed snow and ice below.

Sully felt Syre sitting in front of him, and the Glyph behind.

He couldn't help noticing that neither of them were gripping onto the Day'gatarn's feathers for dear life . . . and he assumed that it had something to do with magic.

From the way that Syre was mumbling something or other beneath her breath, he supposed that she had had some part in preventing the Day'gatarn from tearing Sully into easily digestible chunks for its soon-to-be-born babies.

Although he felt far from comfortable on the Day'gatarn's back, he did manage to shift a glance over his shoulder; to the Horrox's tunnels that he had left behind.

All he could see was the tidy, black hole from which they had —*apparently*—emerged.

When Sully turned his attention back to his new surroundings, he couldn't help but notice that night had fallen. He wondered how long he had spent down there, in the Horrox's tunnels. And that was when he heard the Glyph's voice in his brain:

— *The cave is just along here.*

Sully had no idea how the Glyph could tell anything at all about their surroundings.

The darkness, at least to Sully, was complete.

And yet, in the dim glow of the moon from above, he *could* make out the distant talons of the Day'gatarn below; and how it picked its way effortlessly across the packed layers of snow below them, as if guided by some sense of direction which Sully had no chance of even understanding the beginning of.

When Sully turned his attention forward, he saw over Syre's shoulder to the Creature's enormous beak, and how it bowed its head with each of its strides, seemingly putting more effort into each subsequent bound.

As promised, the Day'gatarn approached a large opening—*a cave*—and Sully felt the Creature thankfully slowing its pace.

It was only when he watched Syre nonchalantly throw herself off the back of the Day'gatarn—surely a drop of more than three times her height—that Sully realised that he would be expected to do the same . . . or else remain up here, on the back of this Day'-gatarn, forevermore.

Sully sensed the Glyph still behind him, apparently not having been struck with the same bravery which Syre had managed to channel.

Or the same stupidity.

The Day'gatarn slowed to a halt, tilted its neck back, and pointed its beak at the stars above them. From somewhere within its enormous, birdlike body, it summoned a mighty *roar*!

Sully's first reaction was to cling on tight to the Day'gatarn's feathers, to squeeze it ever tighter with his knees. But this only proved effective for as long as his strength was able to hold out.

Soon enough, he felt his grip giving way; the vibrations which ploughed through the Day'gatarn's body too much for him to resist.

Although later Sully was certain that either Syre or the Glyph might've had something to do with it, he felt his grip loosening from the feathers and his whole body tumbling downward—*very fast*—to the hard-packed snow and ice below.

Sully didn't have enough time to get his limbs in the right position.

He ended up landing on his backside.

The pain jangled up his spine, and he felt a brief flashback to the pain which'd wracked his body back in the Horrox's tunnels.

The memories were the worst of it.

And he soon managed to get shot of them as soon as he caught sight of Syre's wry smile, and saw that she extended a helping hand to him.

Taking her hand, Sully returned to an upright position. He

glanced back at the Day'gatarn. It had given up its roaring for the time being.

Instead, it stirred its talons in the snow.

Jets of warm breath blasted out of its beak.

Without warning, the Day'gatarn suddenly lurched off its mark and galloped away from them, soon becoming lost to the darkness which surrounded the mouth of the cave.

Sully turned into Syre and the Glyph, seeing their expressions of slight amusement.

Sully couldn't help but shake his head. "I suppose we're not going to stop it?"

Syre and the Glyph smiled back at him by way of reply, then Syre answered, "No, we only wanted to see what we were dealing with."

"In what way?" Sully replied.

Syre glanced to the Glyph, and then looked to Sully. "From what we've gathered, from the news we've heard spreading throughout the Winter's Moan, the Horrox are preparing for war; they're going to launch a strike on Ilsnare."

Sully felt his chest tighten.

Just as he'd imagined it . . . more war was coming.

A question continued to linger on Sully's mind.

And since he realised that he couldn't look any more ridiculous than he had when he'd taken the tumble off the Day'gatarn's back just now, he decided there was no harm in asking it.

"Why did you need me to act as 'bait' ?"

Syre and the Glyph exchanged glances.

Syre replied, "We suspected that the Horrox, resident nearby, were controlling the Day'gatarn somehow." She paused for a long moment. "Although you might be surprised to think it by its appearance, the Day'gatarn is a somewhat peaceable Creature . . . and we believed the Horrox to be controlling its mind and that if we were just to follow it back to its nest it would lead us to the Horrox's lair."

Sully stared back at the two of them. "And you got what you wanted?"

A slight smirk crossed Syre's lips. "We found the location of the Horrox's lair, yes, and we managed to listen into their thoughts; to discover the exact nature of their plans."

"And what are they?" Sully said, glancing to the Glyph for a moment.

"They plan on a sneak-attack on Ilsnare," Syre replied. "For them to get in underneath the City Walls and then to turn the place upside down; to strike fear into the citizens. From what we could understand"—here Syre slipped the Glyph a sidelong glance—"there have been reports sweeping through the Horrox of a massacre in the south of the Kingdom; a massacre of Horrox by Mortals."

Sully couldn't help but frown slightly at this. To tell the truth he couldn't see why *anyone* wouldn't take those delightful Creatures to their bosom . . . at least he still had his sense of humour.

He knew that he would be waking from nightmares for the remainder of his natural life, believing that he might be about to suffer from that same pain all over again.

At the hands of the Horrox.

Feeling his mind getting the better of him, and deciding to turn his concentration back onto what faced them in the immediate future, Sully said, "So, where to next?"

Syre's expression straightened out.

Again, she glanced to the Glyph.

Then back to Sully.

"We've decided that it's best to return—to *warn* the others." Syre paused for a long moment as if she had trouble just *speaking* the next line. "To return to Ilsnare."

Sully felt as if an invisible weight grew in the air, over their heads, and since he couldn't think of any way he might be able to mitigate it, he decided to change the subject.

"What's for dinner?" he said, vaguely directing the question at the Glyph.

The Glyph smirked. "Depends what you can catch," it said, and then promptly disappeared in a puff of smoke.

Sully stared at the empty air where the Glyph had once been.

Then he looked to Syre.

She, too, had disappeared.

For what felt almost like an eternity, Sully crossed his arms over his chest in some vague attempt to keep the chill out of his too-thin tunic. He'd been waiting there for five minutes or more when he decided that he should enter the cave and spark up a fire; the fact that he had nothing with which to achieve this didn't register for the first few moments.

And when it did, he let loose a frustrated, long-winded *groan*.

A groan which was almost immediately swallowed by the buffeting wind.

It was then that Sully turned to look around him.

And saw Syre, and the Glyph, standing nearby.

Neither of them able to contain themselves.

Despite shaking his head, and generally trying to look as disapproving as possible, Sully couldn't help but feel just a little gladness that they *had* returned . . . that they hadn't left him out in the Winter's Moan to freeze to death.

Life was all about the small mercies.

By the time Syre had handed him her fire-lighting kit, and Sully had done a good job at getting a campfire blazing, he couldn't help but feel glad that he would have company back out of the Winter's Moan.

As for all this business about a coming war, Sully wasn't so sure that he would commit himself *just yet* . . . he was getting older with each and every passing season after all . . .

But that was a matter to be sorted out another day.

For now, he could see that the Glyph had once more made itself scarce from the cave; that it had apparently gone off to search for their dinner. He wondered, when the Glyph came back, whether he should ask about *its* gender . . . if it had one at all.

In the meantime, while Sully waited, it was just him and Syre —on opposing sides of the campfire—both of them staring into the flames.

The two of them—*clearly*—thinking about very different things.

51

THE PALACE CATACOMBS

F LUCKNOR LISTENED to the stone crumbling all around him.

He felt chunks of it brush against his cheek.

His whole body was tense. It felt as if his muscles might burst through his skin.

His heart beat in his mouth.

Darkness reigned over everything.

When Flucknor dared to open his eyes, he saw that same neon-blue glow illuminating the Palace Library. But all he could make out were blurred, twisted, shadowy figures.

He watched on as the bright clouds of light were tossed back and forth; between the bookshelves, ducking and diving as they went on to—*invariably*—miss their target.

He waited for the bright cloud intended for him.

But it never came.

He waited for it . . . and *waited* . . . but it never arrived.

That was when Flucknor noted the etched stone which they'd attempted to shift before.

That it had been destroyed by the first hex.

Flucknor glanced back, into the Library, to the figures as they continued their melee.

He wondered what he might do to aid them and came up empty.

His lack of magical knowledge—quite simply—made him more of a liability than anything else. He wouldn't be anywhere near able to compete with the others.

Even if he tried to cast some enchantment or other, he was certain that the two Creatures and the Great Mage would be able to bat it away with ease; as if it was nothing more deadly than a drop of rain.

It was then that he made his decision.

He looked to the wide-open hole in the wall, and decided he should go down.

The others could join him later.

In the Palace Catacombs.

52

DARKNESS

F LUCKNOR HAD PREPARED HIMSELF for the stink of the Catacombs; for the dankness he was certain would cling to every part . . . and for the rodents which might skitter about his feet.

What he hadn't prepared himself for, however, was the darkness.

It probed and pressed at him from all sides.

Seemingly never-ending.

Seemingly *all-consuming.*

As it turned out, a staircase ran down from the other side of the entrance into the Palace Library.

He wondered to himself—still hearing the crashes and explosions caused by the misdirected hexes and enchantments—whether this route had once been a standard one . . . one which hadn't been hidden behind that large stone engraving.

He had never investigated much of the Palace history; the few tomes he had bothered to pick up he had found to be so vaingloriously inflected—so swept up in their own *grandeur* of past victories—that he had been unable to work out what approximation of the truth remained within them.

Several of the stories he'd read about the stone etching had described it as being present there in the Palace ever since it had been constructed—another date which was hotly contested depending on the source.

Whether or not it had always been located in the Library was where Flucknor would concentrate his research if it ever came to that...

Right now, though, he was fighting to escape the magical battle raging above.

Flucknor trod down the staircase, feeling the cool surface of the stone wall to guide his way. Over his shoulder, he heard a large *crash* but didn't stop or turn to look.

He listened to the rubble—the apparent fallout of the magical strike—tumble down after him. He wondered whether or not—supposing they came through the melee—Brotsboore and Rintersyart would be able to pursue him down the stairs.

What if—during the battle—the hole in the Library wall had become blocked?

Flucknor knew it was impossible to turn back.

Lou would destroy him.

Finally, Flucknor reached the base of the staircase, and he turned back to look up the stairs. He could just make out the faint glimmer of moonlight passing through the gap in the wall above. And he still heard the percussive noises of the hexes and enchantments swirling through the air ... and he felt the ice in his blood tingling away.

He waited for that tug; that *urge* within him to drag him back up the staircase, to aid Lou.

Wasn't that what Lou had kept him near for?

So that Flucknor would come running to protect him whenever necessary?

But Flucknor felt no urge.

Only the Mortal sense that he had to flee in terror.

Once Flucknor had got several paces through the Catacombs, he began to wonder if Lou was there at all. He had never seen his face—never seen the person who had thrown the hex . . . and Flucknor had felt no desire to return and protect his 'master'.

Could it be that another mage had leaped in to defend the Palace?

He continued on his way, afraid of what might really be happening.

The next time he stopped it was because he heard—with a low *splash*—his boot land in a stream.

Quickly, he felt the damp sensation spread through the hole in the toe of his boot, and then through his sock. Only when he looked up did he realise he wasn't alone.

There, standing before him, was Lou.

His face lit up with the neon-blue glow of ice magic.

Flucknor stared back into Lou's face, unable to square with himself just what he was witnessing; unable to get his logical brain to kick into some sort of order.

As he heard the magical battle continue to rage above his head —in the Palace Library—he knew that Louson Dorf—allpowerful mage; and King of Shellacnass—stared back at him. And although Flucknor knew that he should run, he couldn't bring himself to take the first step.

He was completely paralysed.

From head to toe.

Lou stared back at him, then tilted his head to one side. "You can't understand it—can you?"

If Flucknor had been able to do so, he might've acknowledged that Lou's presumption was correct. But he couldn't so much as twitch a fingertip.

Lou continued, taking a step closer to him. "I don't suppose that Gdandra ever got around to any of the more *select* enchant- ments—nothing like *self-replication*?"

Flucknor's brain stretched.

He saw it now . . . or, at least, he *thought* he could see it.

"While I speak with you here," he said, "I'm also fighting with those Creatures up in the Library. A very difficult ability to master, I'm sure you'll appreciate, and one which takes a *huge* amount of energy to achieve." Lou glanced over Flucknor's head, to the staircase leading up to the Library. "In fact, I don't believe I shall be able to hold it very much longer at all; I should get to the point."

Still, Flucknor felt himself frozen in place.

It was as if half a dozen invisible hands held him:

At his ankles, at his wrists, about his neck.

Lou crept even closer to Flucknor, bringing his nose so near that their tips almost brushed. "I want to know why you're leaving —why you decided that this is the only way."

Flucknor felt the invisible hand about his throat release its grip.

He stared Lou in the eye and felt a harsh, frozen stirring in his stomach.

There was no point in lying now.

He might as well tell Lou the whole truth if he was to die in any case.

"You burned it down," Flucknor said. "The Great Hall—you killed all those people; all those members of the Council of Wisemen."

Lou held Flucknor's gaze for a long while, and then said, almost as if it was punctuation rather than words, "Go on."

Flucknor continued, "*Why*? Why did you do it?"

Lou held himself very still, and then he turned his gaze away, to look out into the gloom which surrounded them. "It was a test, Flucknor; I had to be sure that you had it in you . . . that you'd become aligned totally with the light." He turned back to Flucknor. "There wasn't any other way, you need to believe me."

But Flucknor wouldn't hear of it.

Lou could regurgitate all the justifications in the world and it would never compensate for what he had done. Flucknor could only think back to the stories he had heard, about how Lou had killed one of the previous Kings of Shellacnass while he lay in bed . . . when Flucknor had first heard the story he had been almost unable to understand it in the context of the Lou who he knew.

Now, though, it seemed easier to believe.

In fact, it seemed only *logical.*

Realising that he had only death to look forward to now, and that he might as well get everything out on the table, he said, "All these years you kept me close without ever having the courtesy to tell me why; to tell me that you wanted me to be your own personal protector. Why didn't you say anything? Why didn't you ever teach me about the magic which runs through my veins like you promised?"

Lou was looking away, shaking his head, as if there was some universal truth he would simply never be able to understand . . . some kind of a truth which was *beyond* Flucknor to understand.

More than anything else, Flucknor longed to reach out and give Lou a good shake.

To wake him from his delusions.

Lou still held himself away from Flucknor, again seemingly occupied within his own thoughts.

Then he said, "Because I wasn't able; I was *afraid* . . . afraid that I might corrupt your alignment."

He looked back at Flucknor, meeting his eye.

"I searched for the right one to guide you for so long, and I only found her recently: Gdandra. If you need help now, you know where you should go." He paused for a second, and then added, "As for you being my own personal protector, although it's up to you whether or not to believe me, that was never my intention."

Above their heads there was an enormous explosion—louder than any which had come before. The two of them turned their attention upward.

When the reverberations following the explosion ceased, Lou turned back to Flucknor and said, "It was never my intention to make you my prisoner; to treat you like you were some sort of a criminal, but please believe me that I only wished to keep you close. Now I can see, though, that the safest place for you shall be outside the City Walls . . . far from me."

Flucknor felt his heart beating harder.

He wasn't quite sure he understood what Lou said.

That Flucknor wasn't to be put to death.

And yet, he had believed that to be the only option.

From that moment onward, it all happened quickly.

Flucknor saw the flash of white light.

At first he believed it to be a hex which Lou had cast.

Then he felt Lou tumbling toward him, into his chest.

It was only when Flucknor's arms came to embrace Lou that he realised the truth.

That he was dead.

53

GREEN PASTURES

S ULLY FELT the warming winds of the plains up ahead.

Although he saw no end to the ice fields, he was *certain* that they were just around the corner from leaving the Winter's Moan behind . . . hopefully for good.

For the first time in what felt like *years*, he could feel that a workman's sweat had broken out on his brow. And that the thin tunic which he wore underneath was sticking to his skin. Ever since Sully had set out, he had regretted the equipment he had brought along with him into the Winter's Moan . . . that it had either been insufficient or *wildly* unsuitable.

But he would soon be out.

And, all going well, he would be back home.

He heard his stomach give a *groan*.

Despite the Glyph's best efforts, the hunting had been slim-pickings these last few days. The Glyph often made excuses about how the animals had already headed south to the grassy plains.

As for Sully, he couldn't help wondering if the Glyph was taking a breather from having kept him alive for the past—whoever *knew* how many—days.

Albeit the Glyph had put Sully to good use as 'bait'.

Sully trudged onward, listening to the gentle footfalls of Syre and the Glyph, both of them a few paces back.

The next step was just like any other, there was no reason for Sully to believe it any different . . . it was—however—*totally* different; because, as he took it, he brought the first, long scrap of green into sight; the first piece of land without a frosting of either snow or ice.

Sully was sure that he made a fool of himself, calling out to Syre and the Glyph, pointing wildly at the spot which was just up ahead. Despite the fatigue which'd set in on his body, he felt lively now, as if he had energy to go ahead and do it all again.

Well, perhaps he *did* have the energy, but whether he had the will was another matter altogether.

The greenery up ahead seemed to have a positive effect on all three of them, as their pace increased. Bringing more and more of the green pastures into sight. Already, Sully could make out the grazing cows and sheep, spotted on the hillsides. The occasional countryside cottage sprinkled here and there.

Already, Sully found his mind becoming overwhelmed with all the trimmings of civilisation; fresh milk and butter; easy-to-procure meat . . . no longer would he be dependent on the Glyph's offerings. No longer would he have to live like a baby; coddled from the wind and cold, offered a nipple before bedtime. He felt almost as if he was *alive* all over again.

It was only when Sully set foot on the lush, long grass as it swayed in the warm, southern wind, that he found himself turning his attention back to Syre and the Glyph.

Taking the two of them in.

Both wore wide smiles.

Both seemed just as eager to take in all they could of this fresh terrain stretching out before them.

When Syre and the Glyph joined Sully in rejoicing at the first sprouting of long grass at their feet, Sully couldn't help but sense the nagging tone at the back of his mind. The one which was asking him what would become of them now. What would become of their *friendship*.

With this in mind, Sully turned his attention onto the Glyph.

And it seemed, even though he didn't have the ability to read minds, that the Glyph's thoughts were cast over more or less the same issues.

"Well," Sully began, breaking the silence, and then looking to the Glyph. "What do you plan on doing now that you've shepherded us safely from the Winter's Moan?"

The Glyph's round eyes froze onto Sully's. "I was wondering if I should begin charging Mortals for the privilege."

Even though the joke was somewhat staid for Sully's tastes—and considering that he had spent a goodly, or badly, amount of time around Royal Guards, it wasn't hard to see why—he couldn't help but smile from ear to ear.

A silence descended on the group, and Sully found himself slipping Syre a sidelong glance. She continued to stare across the horizon, as if she might be able to make out Ilsnare.

"So," Sully said, again the one charged with thawing the conversation, "is there anything remaining for us in the Winter's Moan—anything that we should bring back to Ilsnare?"

Neither Syre or the Glyph said anything.

Sully supposed that, really, there wasn't anything to say at all.

And, no doubt, Syre and the Glyph had extremely important matters on their mind.

Finally, it was Syre who turned to Sully, a slight smile lacing her lips, as she said, "I *was* wondering if we were going to travel the entire distance by foot."

Sully smiled back at her. "That depends," he said. "Got any money on you?"

Syre reached back behind her. She gave her rucksack a faithful pat. "I think there'll be enough to get us back . . . you don't think my brother would've cast me out into the wilderness with nothing but a pair of grung to rub together, do you?"

Sully felt a warmth descend on him.

When he turned his attention upward, he saw that the sun had emerged from between the frumpy, black-bottomed clouds. The rays warmed his blood; warded away all those unpleasant, frozen memories.

Memories which—for good or ill—would remain with him for the rest of his days.

"All right, then," Syre said, a slight sigh to her voice. She nodded to the nearest cottage. "Let's go see if they have any horses to sell us, shall we?"

Syre and the Glyph moved off their spots, taking further steps into the long grass of the plains, at the same time leaving Sully rooted where he was; still standing behind the line which divided the Winter's Moan from the verdant plains of Shel-lacnass.

He couldn't help but shift a final glance over his shoulder, to the looming hills, all of them iced with snow. He wondered whether; today, or tomorrow . . . next week, these hillsides would be spotted with advancing Horrox armies.

And then he began to wonder who there might be to prevent their advance.

He turned his attention back to the plains; the road which would lead him home.

One thing was for certain, he and Syre would be among those to stand up against evil; and, from the look of things, it seemed that the Glyph would stand up and be counted among them also.

Sully shifted off his spot, treading over the plains, pushing matters like that from his mind for the time being. This was a time for celebration; not for pensiveness.

He broke into a trot, already seeing that Syre and the Glyph had advanced far ahead. When he reached them, he couldn't help but notice the wide smile which now sat easily across his lips.

Because they—*all of them*—were finally going home.

54

A DEAD KING

F LUCKNOR FELT HIMSELF shaking all over.

His mind couldn't get around the reality.

That Lou's head—his *lifeless* body—leaned up against his own.

It sent a quiver to the pit of his gut. A shimmer passed through his blood.

Almost as if the world was responding to Flucknor's thoughts, his gaze rose up above Lou's corpse, and beyond; out into the shadows of the Catacombs.

Standing there, he saw Brotsboore.

His red skin glowing gently.

The eyes which'd once been pit-black now nothing but a brilliant white.

His hands were exposed from the sleeves of his robe.

And the tips of his fingers matched his eyes.

Brotsboore spoke into Flucknor's mind:

— *We need to go. Lou has managed to kill me.*

Flucknor again felt his mind twist into knots.

He wondered if what Brotsboore had wanted to say was the reverse, but it didn't seem like now was the time to split hairs.

Brotsboore turned, his skin shedding the dim, red glow all about the Catacombs, lighting their way. It was now that Flucknor could properly make out their surroundings; that he could see that the Catacombs were designed almost like a canal: two walkways on either side with a dug-out trench down the middle.

Flucknor's gaze shifted over the occasional puddle of water which reflected Brotsboore's glowing skin. Before proceeding on Brotsboore's heels, Flucknor flashed a final glance back over his shoulder. And then it struck him.

Due to shock, he spoke aloud, rather than directly into Brotsboore's mind.

"What about Rintersyart?! We left him behind—in the Library!"

Brotsboore didn't break his pace and when his words appeared in Flucknor's mind, they seemed calm and collected. As if he wasn't disturbed at all by this piece of information.

— *Rintersyart is dead. Gone. And he won't be the last casualty of the war. Not by a long stretch.*

Flucknor continued to stare back over their shoulders, back toward the staircase which led up to the Library. He felt his heart throbbing in his chest and the ice magic in his blood prickled his veins. He wondered if he could keep on going—if his feet wouldn't simply give out beneath him . . . but he continued to put one foot in front of the other; determined to keep on going. He worried that if he stopped—even for one second—he would never be able to start again.

He followed Brotsboore, not even pausing to wonder how

Brotsboore now appeared to understand the way out of the City Walls . . . how to get beyond them.

On one occasion, Flucknor noticed what he believed to be light.

And promptly watched as Brotsboore steered off along a tunnel in the opposite direction.

When he pointed this out—this time remembering to speak within his own mind—Brotsboore said nothing.

He only kept on plodding forward.

Apparently deeper into the Catacombs.

Flucknor judged them to have run through the spiralling, labyrinthine tunnels for five or ten minutes before Brotsboore brought them to a halt before a large, iron door.

Flucknor looked to the door. Besides the rust which grew up off the surface, he couldn't help noticing that there were rivulets of water running between the gaps.

He glanced to Brotsboore, as if looking for an explanation.

Brotsboore gave him one.

— *The River Ils. It's the fastest way out of the city. The only way we can be completely certain that the Royal Guards on watch won't see us flee.*

Flucknor had no time to opine on this theory because Brotsboore was already reaching out for the lever which released the lock on the door.

Yanking it toward him.

There was a moment when Flucknor was certain Brotsboore would be unable to get the door open . . . but then, with a single, solid *jerk*; he managed it.

A torrent of water gushed through the gap.

The foul-smelling River Ils pouring its muddy, brown contents into the Catacombs.

Flucknor stood by wondering if it would ever stop.

What if the entire contents of the river was drained into the Catacombs?

... A pair of shadowy figures venturing along an empty, dried-up riverbed would hardly go unnoticed by the Royal Guards who patrolled the City Walls.

Finally, though, the torrent of water slowed.

Not entirely, but enough so that it no longer filled the entire doorway.

It ran in a steady stream, flushing into the dug-out trenches of the Catacombs; creating subterranean canals.

Even as Brotsboore grabbed hold of his shirt and then spoke into his mind, Flucknor couldn't help wondering just what the function of these canals might be.

— *Come on! We have to be quick!*

Flucknor allowed Brotsboore to tug him from the spot the soles of his boots had nearly rooted him to. He waded after Brotsboore, through the steady stream of the stinking, dark water.

Before they ventured onward, Brotsboore turned back and —*with a fiery orb*—brought his magic to bear on the door behind them.

It closed with an eerie *squeal* of unoiled hinges.

Flucknor could still hear the water trickling about him, and he realised that they needed to work harder to make their way upstream ... the water level would soon rise up above their heads.

Flucknor couldn't help but speak into Brotsboore's mind once more:

— *When will you tell me what happened up in the Library? What happened to Rintersyart? What happened to Lou?*

Flucknor could hear Brotsboore's heavy breathing.

His exertion following the night's events.

Then came his response:

— *I'll tell you . . . in daylight.*

55

IN DAYLIGHT

W HEN THEY EMERGED from the inlet, Flucknor felt as if his entire body might freeze solid.

His entire bottom half—his *trousers*—were soaked right through.

When the night-time breeze blew against him he felt the chill cut him right down to the bone.

He glanced back to the City Walls.

He saw that they loomed above, and that several torches hung down from the sable stonework.

He could make out the silhouettes of a pair of guards patrolling the ramparts.

He ducked his head down, reminding himself to keep his body as close to the surface of the water as possible.

He could feel Brotsboore behind.

The ripples from Brotsboore's berth in the water lightly brushing against him.

Flucknor held his concentration, lightly paddling his way downstream, allowing himself almost to float on the surface of the River Ils; toward the trees which sprouted up from the opposing hillside.

Freedom.

The escape was nothing as Flucknor had imagined. After the showdown with Lou it seemed positively *relaxed*. He had to exercise patience, forcing his body to go slack so he could float himself along the surface of the river; allowing the current to drag him away.

As Flucknor did drift across the surface of the water, his mind entered a state similar to sleep. He found himself seeing images behind his closed eyelids: Gdandra, Lou . . . Syre . . . all of these people in his life; all of those he loved and cared about.

And all those who had—in some way—betrayed him.

For Flucknor couldn't help but feel that the scroll from Gdandra he had received on the day of the fire at the Great Hall hadn't been a total coincidence; that if Flucknor had decided to blow off the meeting with the Council she would only have steered him back.

Back to the Great Hall.

He couldn't shift the feeling that Gdandra, as much as Lou, had wanted to see if Flucknor truly did 'walk in the light' . . . otherwise she might well have been wasting her time . . .

Flucknor allowed his eyelids to flicker open when the sunlight reddened them.

For several seconds, he allowed the sun to dazzle him, and for the ice magic to react to the brightness by itching at his veins, making its protestations at the fire inherent in the sun.

But, even though he might 'walk in the light', he would never forget the lessons which he had picked up second-hand . . . those lessons dispensed from Lou to Syre—from brother to sister . . . about how he had to always remain humble; to 'walk in weakness'.

He wondered what might happen to him if he refused to do so.

If he decided that he would give himself totally to the light.

Would it destroy him; just as other mages had been lost to their magic?

Flucknor supposed that he would see.

If his mastery ever reached the level where it would become an issue.

He heard Brotsboore speak into his mind, and it was only then that he recalled his promise. That Brotsboore would reveal what had happened back at the Palace when the sunlight shone down on them.

— *Lou replicated himself . . . he left a version to fight up in the Library, against me and Rintersyart. When I realised what was happening, I decided that I had to do the same . . . that I had to create another version of myself. I believed that his intention was to cause you harm in some way; that he wanted to murder you while me and Rintersyart were distracted.*

Flucknor felt a pang in his gut to hear the word 'murder' bandied about so readily; as if naming it was enough to resolve all the complications of the matter.

As if it was a clear-cut, *simple* thing.

Brotsboore continued:

— *I replicated myself, turned my attention to pursuing Lou, down in the Catacombs. And I stood in wait, in the shadows. I was certain that he would detect me, but his concentration wasn't complete. He had to fight us back up in the Library, after all. And when I sensed there to be a threat to you, when I believed that Lou was going to kill you I decided to act . . . and I administered a killing curse before he had the chance to do the same to you.*

As Flucknor floated along on his back, staring up at the searing blue sky above, he couldn't help but feel his mind nearly breaking apart; trying to understand all of the angles.

Finally, he managed to reply, speaking the words into Brotsboore's mind:

— *So, Lou isn't dead?*

Brotsboore held off replying for several moments, and Flucknor realised that trees had begun to sprout up from the riverbanks, on both sides.

When Flucknor turned his attention to them, he realised that they had arrived.

That they had reached *freedom* without any further obstacles.

They had managed to escape Ilsnare . . . Flucknor had managed to escape *Lou.*

Brotsboore hauled himself onto the bank and then reached out to help Flucknor up behind him.

Once the two of them lay there, on the bank; both exhausted from the fraught night, Brotsboore finally answered him:

— *Louson is not dead. Up in the Library, he killed my alternate body; just as I killed his down in the Catacombs. Rintersyart, though, was not so lucky.*

Although Flucknor had heard from Brotsboore that Rintersyart was dead, he hadn't yet been able to process the information completely. He found the concept that he was gone . . . that Lou had *killed* him, almost too much to bear.

For several seconds, Flucknor remained reverent, thinking about the fragility of life, and how death was only ever a whisper away . . . he would never forget *that* particular lesson if he hadn't learned it well enough already.

Finally, another thought struck Flucknor, from the night before.

He spoke it to Brotsboore:

— *How did you know which way to go; in the Catacombs? How did you know which way would lead us to that passageway which led out to the Ils?*

Brotsboore remained silent for a long while, and when Flucknor cast a glance in his direction, he saw that a gentle smile rested over his lizard's snout; over his lizard's *lips.*

This time Brotsboore spoke aloud, as if a masterstroke such as this demanded to be felt in the physical world. "Soon after Lou had killed Rintersyart, when Lou stood over me, when the killing curse sparked away at his fingertips, he whispered the instructions to me in a low voice; the instructions of how we were to escape."

Flucknor felt an immediate and strong tightness wrap about his chest.

He felt a skitter pass through his blood.

His ice magic . . . or his lightness . . . alerting him to something or other.

Flucknor shook his head. "I don't understand."

"Don't you see?" Brotsboore said, smiling more widely now. "He knew that I had created another version of myself; that I was down there, in the gloom of the Catacombs, biding my time in the darkness." Brotsboore paused another moment and then added, as if it needed mentioning at all, "Louson wanted you to escape— he wanted you to *know* how to escape. It was his plan all along. For me to kill the form of himself down in the Catacombs. And, all the while, up in the Library, he would be victorious."

Although Flucknor felt as if he should smile back at Brots-boore—if only to be polite—he couldn't even raise the strength to fake it.

He felt an overwhelming sickness grow within him.

Because he couldn't help but believe that—*somehow*—he was still doing Lou's bidding.

Was he really so predictable that Lou could utilise him as a pawn?

. . . Over and over and *over* again?

Flucknor lay very still, feeling the gentle, warm breeze blowing over the plains; the breeze from the south. He listened to the long grasses swish about as the wind caught them.

He knew that today was shaping up to be blazing hot; that it would be one of the many markers of the summer to come.

There was something about the stillness of their surroundings —perhaps it was the early hour—but Flucknor couldn't quite bring himself to feel comfortable.

To completely allow his muscles to relax.

And the magic in his blood certainly wouldn't allow him to relax.

It continued to throb about his veins.

To squeeze his stomach.

But what was it trying to tell him?

Was it trying to tell him anything at all?

. . . He wondered if he hadn't played the part of the naïve apprentice, leaving the shelter of his master before time . . . leaving *Lou's* shelter . . . because, no matter what Lou himself said, about his unsuitability to fulfil the master's role for Flucknor—and that Gdandra would be his best bet—he knew that Lou would always be his master.

Flucknor felt the warmth of the sunrays warming his blood, and, at the same time, he felt the slight chill through his chest. He knew that it was impossible for him to know, for sure, whether or not he had done the right thing.

What even *was* the right thing?

He turned back to Brotsboore. "What next?" Flucknor said.

"You mean, 'Where will we bed down for the night?' " Brotsboore replied, a slight smile lining his lips.

Flucknor shook his head. "No," he said. "I mean, what happens *next* . . . with the struggle? What can I do to help?"

Brotsboore's smile widened. "You still wish to help us, even after all that has gone on, all that has happened?"

Flucknor thought about the Great Hall burning down.

All those people fleeing.

Without a doubt, he knew Ilsnare would be on its knees before long, what with all but one member of the Council of Wisemen disposed of.

And then Ilsnare would be beneath Lou's watch.

Gods help them . . .

How many would be injured—*killed*—in the process?

Flucknor turned his attention away from the pit-black walls which surrounded Ilsnare; the Crystal City . . . the glass rooftops all shimmering in the rising, golden sunlight.

He looked to Brotsboore, and then said, "Yes, I'll stand with you."

For a long moment, the smile faded from Brotsboore's lips, and he, in turn, shifted his attention to the Crystal City as it stood up from the plains before them.

And then he said, "There's a war coming, you know?"

Even though this was the first Flucknor had heard of it

described in such tones, he couldn't help but feel that Brotsboore was correct.

He had *felt* it in the air.

Brotsboore reached up with his claws, away from Ilsnare, and then drew an invisible line on the landscape, to the north of the city. "They'll be coming down from the Winter's Moan—*my people* . . . they've been stirring restlessly for years, hidden out of sight, but now is the time for them to return to these promised lands." He shifted his attention fully onto Flucknor once again. "Whoever thought to believe that these lands should only belong to Mortals?"

Flucknor felt a knot form in his throat.

He swallowed it back.

"You do realise what this means," Brotsboore said, "that you'll end up a traitor among your own people; that if this fails you might never be able to walk among Mortals again?"

Flucknor gave a slight nod. "Yes," he said, "I understand that."

Brotsboore parted his lips as if to add something else, but, in the end, he remained silent, and the two of them sat on the bank of the Ils watching the dawn taking hold of the landscape; growing day out of the darkened soil of night.

It was in those moments that Flucknor realised only one thing was for certain now.

For the foreseeable future, he would stand at Brotsboore's side —at the side of the Creatures; of the Horrox; *all* Magical beings.

He would aid them in their strife for freedom.

And for equality.

This would be his true Galleries of Justice.

The place where he could make a *real* difference in the world.

56

THE THRONE ROOM

LOUSON DORF sat upon his throne feeling the sunlight streaming over him.

He felt its golden, warming rays bringing the ice in his veins almost to the boil.

His heart hummed in his chest.

And his whole body was wracked with fatigue following the melee of the night before.

A fraught occasion.

Some days, when he woke, he felt frail—as if his relatively youthful body had been replaced with that of an elderly man in the middle of the night. Most mornings, he expected to peer into the mirror and see the wrinkled skin sagging down from his throat.

It was often a surprise to see that his youth still remained with him.

That only a few white flashes in his hair betrayed his otherwise youthful appearance.

Lou dragged his gaze across the marble, emerald floor of the Throne Room. His eyes settled on the pile of leathered tomes all stacked up; their pages encrusted with dust and yellowed from constant thumbing. Sometimes he couldn't bear to wonder how long he had spent among those pages, among line upon line of scrawling, pit-black ink.

Some days it made him nauseous.

Like today.

But he could still think . . . *think* about the contents of those books; and the dream which they had instilled in him; the dream for a fairer kingdom, one in which all types of beings would be able to walk in freedom and equality. And yet, he sensed the impatience— the tormented *impatience*—for everything to fall into place right now.

As if it was a simple matter of storming the castle and slaying the dragon.

Because that was what they planned to do with him.

From his spies, Lou had heard the news that the Horrox were on the move; that they were heading down from the Winter's Moan; coming for Ilsnare.

But what would that achieve?

If they managed to depose him, what would happen next?

Lou wasn't naïve enough to believe that the Horrox would rule with those admirable virtues of freedom and equality.

First and foremost, as with all races, they would do whatever best suited them.

That would be their priority.

It would be no different from Mortal rule.

No, Lou had a longer-term perspective; and, what was more, he was almost certain that he had a solution. That he had the answer which'd been lacking in Shellacnass for the entirety of history . . . at least he *thought* he did.

It would depend on others . . . others like Flucknor; who, with a heavy heart, he had allowed to leave.

If Flucknor had indeed left—*never to return*—then it presented further troubles.

Ones which might never be reconciled.

And, if that were the case, then Lou would die—nobly, or cowardly; fighting or fleeing—it really wouldn't matter because the Horrox would be those to record history.

Just as the Mortals before them had done the same.

Lou's train of thought was broken by a sharp knock at the door.

He summoned the knocker inside.

He took her in as she darkened the doorway.

Grey hair.

And yet, youthful—*unwrinkled*—skin.

Today, she wore a simple set of beige robes with a silk, pit-black sash tied about the waist.

It was strange to see her without her robes of gold; the crimson tunic beneath.

The dress of the Council of Wisemen.

But the Council no longer existed.

Lou, once again, ruled alone.

Leona; the only member of the Council who had survived the fire at the Great Hall.

Just as Lou had intended it.

Even from across the Throne Room, from his place on the

throne, he could tell that she was trembling; that he *intimidated* her.

Then again, he understood that one of the primary reasons why the people of Ilsnare—the people of Shellacnass—accepted him as their king was because he inspired fear in them.

And they desired Lou to inspire that same sense of fear in Shellacnass's enemies.

But fear couldn't rule forever.

Not once the illusion was broken.

Or a *greater* fear arrived to displace the previous one.

"Your Highness?" Leona said, pausing several paces before the red velvet carpet which led up to his throne.

If Lou had been in a more malevolent mood, he might've insisted that she come several steps closer before she addressed him.

But even he—Louson Dorf, Fearsome Ice Mage—could tell when such shows of power simply weren't necessary.

He had already shown off his strength.

"Do you understand why I let you live?" Lou said, tilting his head slightly to one side.

Leona—the woman who had formerly been the Speaker of the Council of Wisemen—pressed her lips tightly together and clutched her hands at the waistband of her robe. "No, Your Highness."

Despite himself, Lou couldn't help but allow a smile to creep onto his lips. "With all your years of experience you have no idea why you were the only one to survive the fire—the only one who Flucknor thought to save?"

Leona held herself very still so that when she shook her head it was an almost abrupt, uncontrolled movement.

Lou gave a slight pout before shifting back to his previous, neutral expression. "You never realised you were the only Mortal on the Council of Wisemen—the only one who had no magic running through their blood?"

Again, Leona shook her head.

Lou didn't quite know whether or not he should believe her.

Not that it mattered.

"How would you feel," Lou continued, "if I asked you to take on the role of High Representative?"

Leona blinked once—*twice*—and then several times more, as if the glare from the sunlight which beamed in through the glass roof was too much for her to bear.

Then she said, "But, sire, I . . . the Council, there's no longer a place . . . I don't see . . ."

Lou held up his palm. "We'll sort out the details later. What I want now is an answer. Do you accept?" The corner of his mouth —almost without his wishing it to do so—flicked upward to form a wry smile. "Yes, or no?"

Leona stood still for the longest time, and Lou was certain that she wasn't going to be able to respond; that he overawed her to such a degree that his intimidation tactics had sealed her lips.

But then, almost undiscernible, she replied.

"Yes, I accept."

"Good," Lou said, rising up from his throne, pacing over to the pile of books.

When he reached the pile of books, and had laid his palm flat on the very top tome; feeling the gilt lettering of the title: *Magical Meetings of the Mind: How to Unite the Four Corners of the Magical Fields*, he felt her gaze upon him.

Hitting him right between the shoulder blades.

He turned back to her, lifting up the tome at the same time.

The smile from before returned to his lips. "You may go," he said. "I'm sure there's a great deal to attend to"—he paused for the longest time—"*High Representative.*"

Leona gave him a curt bow of her head, and then, without so much as a word—in the manner of a functionary who knew their place—she trod out of the Throne Room.

Lou waited until he had heard the echo of her footsteps completely fade away down the corridor before he took his place back on the throne.

Then he laid the book across his lap.

Turned the pages.

Back to where he had left off reading.

There was so much more to know.

So much more for him to *understand.*

But there was a glimmer . . . no, *more* than a glimmer . . . there were rays of hope streaming from all parts; just like those which streamed down on him from above, through the windows in the roof of the Throne Room.

The very same ones which stirred his blood.

And which would give him no rest.

Not until the day he died.

AUTHOR'S NOTE

Thank you for taking the time to read one of my books. If you would like to hear about my latest releases you can sign up for my newsletter here: www.raymondsflex.com

Thanks for reading!

Raymond S Flex

Galleries Of Justice
The Sixth Crystal Kingdom Novel

www.ingramcontent.com/pod-product-compliance
Lightning Source LLC
Chambersburg PA
CBHW021003260626
47169CB00006B/1917